continued . . .

D0018000

COLTERS'
PROMISE

MAYA BANKS

BERKLEY SENSATION, NEW YORK

THE BERKLEY PUBLISHING GROUP
Published by the Penguin Group
Penguin Group (USA) Inc.
375 Hudson Street, New York, New York 10014, USA
Penguin Group (Canada), 90 Eglinton Avenue East, Suite 700, Toronto, Ontario M4P 2Y3, Canada
(a division of Pearson Penguin Canada Inc.) • Penguin Books Ltd., 80 Strand, London WC2R 0RL,
England • Penguin Group Ireland, 25 St. Stephen's Green, Dublin 2, Ireland (a division of Penguin
Books Ltd.) • Penguin Group (Australia), 250 Camberwell Road, Camberwell, Victoria 3124, Australia
(a division of Pearson Australia Group Pty. Ltd.) • Penguin Books India Pvt. Ltd., 11 Community
Centre, Panchsheel Park, New Delhi—110 017, India • Penguin Group (NZ), 67 Apollo Drive,
Rosedale, Auckland 0632, New Zealand (a division of Pearson New Zealand Ltd.) • Penguin Books
(South Africa) (Pty.) Ltd., 24 Sturdee Avenue, Rosebank, Johannesburg 2196, South Africa

Penguin Books Ltd., Registered Offices: 80 Strand, London WC2R 0RL, England

This is a work of fiction. Names, characters, places, and incidents either are the product of the author's
imagination or are used fictitiously, and any resemblance to actual persons, living or dead, business
establishments, events, or locales is entirely coincidental. The publisher does not have any control over
and does not assume any responsibility for author or third-party websites or their content.

COLTERS' PROMISE

A Berkley Sensation Book / published by arrangement with the author

PUBLISHING HISTORY
Berkley Sensation mass-market edition / June 2012

Copyright © 2012 by Maya Banks.
Excerpt from *Echoes at Dawn* by Maya Banks copyright © 2012 by Maya Banks.
Cover art by S. Miroque.
Cover photos: "Young Couple" by Andreas Gradin/Shutterstock;
"Landscape" by Subbotina Anna/Shutterstock.
Cover design by Rita Frangie.
Interior text design by Kristin del Rosario.

ISBN: 978-0-425-25862-0

BERKLEY SENSATION®
Berkley Sensation Books are published by The Berkley Publishing Group,
a division of Penguin Group (USA) Inc.,
375 Hudson Street, New York, New York 10014.
BERKLEY SENSATION® is a registered trademark of Penguin Group (USA) Inc.
The "B" design is a trademark of Penguin Group (USA) Inc.

PRINTED IN THE UNITED STATES OF AMERICA

10 9 8 7 6 5 4 3 2 1

ALWAYS LEARNING   **PEARSON**

*For all the readers who have loved and supported
the Colter series from the start.
This is for everyone who wanted "more"
and wanted to see Lily further into
the happy relationship she deserves.*

ACKNOWLEDGMENTS

I can honestly say that I never intended to make *Colters' Woman* into a series. Colters' Legacy happened because readers asked for more. And they kept asking. They persevered, and so I decided to write *Colters' Lady* and *Colters' Daughter*. But even then, readers wanted just a little more. They wanted to see Lily with her three husbands who adored her and they wanted to see her happy and safe. They wanted to see Max and Callie a little further down the road and not so raw from their volatile relationship. But most of all, they wanted to see the original Colters, Holly, Adam, Ethan, and Ryan, and see once more the foundation of the entire Colter family. And that even after so many years, the love that was forged between Holly and her three very special men endures. In so many ways, *Colters' Woman* had a huge impact on my career as a writer, and I can only credit my wonderful readers with that. You guys have made so much possible for me. Every story that's come after. Every opportunity I've had to continue providing you with stories that I hope give you a few hours of enjoyment. I owe all of that to you.

CHAPTER 1

LILY Colter sat in the small waiting room of the doctor's office, glancing nervously out the window that overlooked Main Street in Clyde, Colorado. Across the street was her husband's—one of them— office. Seth was sheriff of the small town.

She'd parked around back because sooner or later, Dillon, another of her husbands, would drive through on his way to his pub, and he'd most certainly see her SUV in front of the doctor's office, which would cause him to barge in, demanding to know if everything was all right.

Michael, the middle Colter brother and the third

man she called husband, was safely ensconced in his own veterinary office outside of town, so she wouldn't need to worry about running into him. Hopefully.

Her stomach simply wouldn't settle and she didn't know if it was because of nerves or because—

She couldn't think of that yet. She closed her eyes and squeezed her fingers into tight balls in her lap. It did no good to borrow trouble. Her mother-in-law, Holly Colter, would be the first to tell her that.

It could be some weird stomach bug. Hadn't there been something going around Clyde in the last week? But her issues had presented themselves long before last week and she knew it.

She was unbelievably tired, she was sick over the most ordinary smells, and her breasts were so tender that the slightest pressure made her wince.

The night before when her husbands had made love to her, it had been all she could do not to cry out—in pain—when they lavished gentle attention on her breasts, and she knew then that she had to confront her denial and see the doctor.

"Lily Colter."

Lily looked up to see the nurse standing in the doorway smiling at her. Slowly, Lily pushed herself from the chair and trudged across the room.

The nurse was bright and bubbly, but then Tina always was. If she noticed that Lily wasn't quite herself, she refrained from prying too much.

When, however, she began to take Lily's vitals and ask routine care questions about the reason for her visit, Lily murmured, "I'll discuss it with Dr. Burton."

Tina didn't pursue the matter. She quietly finished taking Lily's blood pressure and temperature, patted Lily reassuringly on the hand, and then promised that Dr. Burton would be along shortly.

Lily slumped against the chair and eyed the exam table nervously. She was scared, uncertain, and worried over what Dr. Burton would say—what she was certain he *would* say.

A moment later, a light knock sounded and the door pushed open. Dr. Burton stuck his head inside, smiled, and then ambled in.

He took a seat across from Lily at the small table and opened the laptop he used for patient notes and records. He met her gaze over the top of the computer and studied her. "So, what brings you in today, Lily?"

If he noted the oddity of her not having at least one of her husbands or another family member present, he didn't say anything. But then there were some things, as she'd learned, that she had to do alone.

This was one of them.

"I think . . ." She closed her eyes. "I suspect . . . I could be pregnant."

When she reopened her eyes, Dr. Burton's were soft with understanding. But instead of saying anything, offering sympathy or reassurance, he merely nodded and then said, "Well, it seems to me the first thing we ought to do before we go any further is do a pregnancy test. Wouldn't you agree?"

She nodded.

"Have you performed an over-the-counter test? Those things are pretty accurate."

She shook her head. "I came here first."

"Well, it won't take but a moment. I'll get Tina back in here. She'll have you give her a urine specimen. If it turns out you're pregnant, then we'll go from there. No sense getting all het up for nothing, right?"

She took in a shaky breath. "No, you're right."

He patted her on the hand and then rose. He leaned out the door and bellowed down the hall for Tina. A moment later, Tina returned, rolling her eyes at the elderly doctor.

She showed Lily into the bathroom and gave her the instructions, which Lily didn't really need, but she stared blankly and nodded as if she had no clue what was expected of her.

Maybe she should have just done one of those stick pregnancy things. At least then she would be home, alone, and not in front of someone else when she received the shock of her life.

A few moments later, she exited the bathroom and returned to her tiny exam room to wait. And wait. Each minute that ticked by seemed like an eternity. She kept eyeing her phone nervously, knowing that eventually someone would figure out she wasn't at home and would want to know what she was up to. And she hated lying. But what was she supposed to say? If she said she was at the doctor's, she'd have no fewer than three people in the waiting room for her when she got out. If she lied and then someone saw her and casually mentioned her whereabouts, it would be even messier.

She sighed, leaned her head down onto the table, and closed her eyes.

Breathe. Just breathe, Lily. They promised it would be different. They swore what happened with Rose wouldn't happen again.

Tears gathered, stinging her eyes and drawing up her nose. She'd gained so much strength during the last two years. Strength she hadn't imagined she possessed. A newfound happiness and independence she would have thought beyond her reach.

But this . . . This had the power to destroy her all over again.

The door opened.

She yanked her head up to meet Dr. Burton's gaze. She stared hard, trying to see something. Some sign.

He came in and sat across from her, his expression still unreadable. Some of the tension started to unknot in her stomach until he reached over to slide his wrinkled hand over hers. He squeezed and her world tilted sideways.

"Lily, my dear, you are indeed pregnant."

Even though she'd known, she'd suspected, the news still came like ice-cold water thrown over her head. Her mouth opened in automatic denial, but she clamped her lips shut and dug her teeth into the bottom one to prevent the sound of dismay from escaping.

Dr. Burton's eyes softened in sympathy. "I know the news isn't ideal and probably not what you wanted to hear. But is it so bad?"

Lily's eyes watered. "I don't understand. I was so careful. I took all my pills." Her cheeks colored at the next admission, but he was her doctor and they'd certainly been down this road before. "We don't use condoms anymore. Maybe I should have insisted we continue. I know they would have done anything for me. But I'd hoped after I started on birth control that we wouldn't need to."

The doctor squeezed her hand again. "Birth control isn't one hundred percent effective. It's close, but you'd be surprised at how many 'oops' babies I've delivered over the years. Sometimes these things just happen, and I'm always convinced that if God intends it, then he finds a way for it to happen. Maybe this baby was just meant to be."

And Rose wasn't?

She wanted to scream it. Why was this baby more deserving of a chance than her sweet, darling daughter had been?

She pushed her knuckles to her mouth and rocked back and forth, desperately trying to maintain control and hold back her grief before it exploded out of her.

Dr. Burton sighed. "I'm going to write a script for some vitamins, and I want you to start taking them. You'll also need to make another appointment on your way out. I want to draw some blood before you leave just so we can take a look at things. My suggestion is to take a few days and think this over. Don't react in the moment. Give it some time to settle in and then you might see that it's not such a bad thing after all. You know those boys will be all over you, and their parents won't be any different. You'll have help, Lily. You won't face this alone."

"Thank you," she murmured. She even tried to return his reassuring smile, but she failed miserably.

The rest of the visit was a blur. Tina came in and drew several vials of blood before handing her a prescription along with some samples of prenatal vitamins that she wanted Lily to start on right away.

"And if you're still taking your birth control pills, you need to discontinue those immediately," Tina said.

Lily nodded numbly, only wanting to get out so she could breathe again.

A few moments later she stumbled out of the doorway into the brisk, cold morning. Her breath escaped in a visible puff and she stood there a long moment, gulping in the chilly air.

Then, realizing she was standing on the sidewalk for anyone to see, she hurried around the corner of the building to the small parking lot in the back where she'd parked her SUV.

After she climbed in, she started the engine but didn't turn on the heat. Her fingers curled around the steering wheel, and for the longest time she simply stared forward out of the windshield. Then she lowered her forehead to the steering wheel as hot tears rolled down her cheeks.

CHAPTER 2

CALLIE Wilder trudged into her house, dropped her purse onto the floor, and promptly flopped onto the couch. Face-first. She groaned once but couldn't summon the energy to adjust her position. She was so tired, and she felt like complete and utter crap.

She wished Max were here. She missed him dreadfully. Especially now that she'd come down with the creeping crud, and all she really wanted to do was curl into his arms and sleep for about a week.

He didn't often go anywhere without her. One of the benefits of being married to a man who had a

Midas touch when it came to business and investments was that she could often indulge in one of her greatest passions. Traveling. And Max was every bit as much of a free spirit as Callie was herself. It was how they met. Only Callie had been backpacking through Europe and Max . . . Well, he had much more luxurious accomodations than she'd had. But that had all changed soon enough.

From the moment they'd met, there was an undeniable spark between them. She'd been drawn to him, found him irresistible. He'd taken over, lavished luxury on her, and she'd spent every available moment with him in his hotel suite.

The only problem was that their meeting hadn't been accidental at all. Max had targeted her and purposely seduced her. All over a piece of land that he considered his legacy.

Just remembering had the power to send shadows through her mind. She hated that the way they met and the wonderful month they'd spent together was forever tainted because it hadn't been real, even though Max swore he'd fallen hard for her from the start.

He'd come for her, all the way to Clyde where she'd sought refuge in the bosom of her loving family. Thus had begun the long, rocky climb to where they were today. Happily married. Forgiveness given. It hadn't been easy, but looking back, Callie knew she didn't regret a single moment because everything that had happened had brought her to where she was today. Stronger. Loved.

Happy.

No, he didn't often go anywhere without her at all, but his sister had called, and Max had left suddenly, worried and quiet. The worry aspect didn't bother Callie so much. Max was a born worrier when it came to the people he loved. But the quiet part was what bugged her. He hadn't said a word. He'd simply told her he had to go and then left.

That had been two days ago. He'd called but he hadn't volunteered what the issue was and she hadn't pushed. She'd find out when he returned even if she had to drag it out of him.

He was getting better about not being so close-mouthed about personal stuff, but he was still a clam. Callie was working on him.

Her cell phone rang, and she groaned again because she didn't want to move in order to answer it. But it was one of her brothers calling—they all had the same ringtone—and if she didn't answer, they'd only worry and come out to check on her.

She fumbled with her pocket and finally dug the phone out, putting it to her ear while she still lay facedown.

"'Lo," she mumbled.

"How are you, baby girl?"

Dillon. Just hearing his voice sent warmth through her chilled veins. Of all her brothers—and she loved them all dearly—she and Dillon were most alike. The rebels or free spirits of the bunch. She'd always shared a closeness with Seth, a bond that she treasured, but she and Dillon had been cut from the same mold.

"Tired," she said, not even bothering to lie and say fine. If it had been Michael or Seth, she could have gotten away with the lie, but Dillon had tossed her out of the bar bright and early, and he knew she didn't look good.

She could hear him frowning through the phone.

"I think you should come over here until Max gets back. Let Lily fuss over you. Or if you won't come here, at least go over to Mom's so she can baby you."

As tempting as the suggestion was, she was simply too exhausted to move. Going anywhere would require far more energy than she possessed. She wanted Max and Max wasn't here.

"I'll be fine," she croaked out. "Just tired."

Dillon snorted. "And don't even think about coming back to the bar. You're done. I'll throw your scrawny ass out of here if you show your face."

Callie sighed, not that she'd argue. She only worked in Dillon's bar when Max was gone, which wasn't often. It gave her something to do to pass the time. She knew Max wasn't particularly fond of her working in the bar, but he didn't say anything, which likely killed him.

She and Max . . . Well, they shared a different type of relationship. Which when she considered that her fathers and her brothers all had a very nontraditional relationship with their one wife, her and Max's situation wasn't that eyebrow raising.

Max was dominant. He expected—demanded—submission. Her submission. But he cherished it and her. But just because she willingly chose to submit to him, he never attempted to curb her free spirit. He loved it too much. He often told her that caging someone such as her was to squash everything that made her the woman he loved.

He was dominant, yes, but he spoiled, pampered, and lavished her with so much love and understanding that she simply couldn't imagine her life any other way. His dominance settled her. Provided her a much-needed sanctuary and haven. She was safe with Max. And she was free to be herself because he loved everything she was.

"Going to bed now," she mumbled to Dillon. "Promise."

"Take care of yourself, Callie," Dillon said. "Love you."

"Love you too."

She ended the call and dropped her arm over the edge of the couch. The phone dangled from her fingertips before hitting the floor with a thud.

It was cold. Her chill bumps even had chill bumps. But she was too miserable to get up and get something for the fever she was sure she had.

Going to her mom and dads' place sounded good, but it would require moving. She could call her mom to come over. If she hadn't dropped the phone already. Being babied by Holly Colter would make anyone feel better.

She tucked her hand back underneath her body and then turned to face the inside of the couch. She reached blindly for the blanket that lay over the back of the couch and pulled it down, drawing up her knees so she could huddle under it.

Oh bliss. She closed her eyes and immediately drifted off.

MAX Wilder pulled into his drive and turned off the windshield wipers. The snow was coming down harder, adding to the few inches already accumulated on the ground.

He got out, eager to see Callie again. He didn't spend much time apart from her, but when Lauren had called, and he'd heard the quiet desperation in her voice, his single-minded goal had been to get to her as fast as possible. In retrospect, he should have taken Callie. It would have been good for Lauren to have Callie there. He hadn't thought. He'd simply reacted and had done as he'd always done. Gone immediately to protect his family.

Only now his family went beyond Lauren. Their mother had passed just a few years earlier, leaving Max and Lauren alone. He'd always been fiercely protective of both his mom and his sister, and he'd been used to being a lone wolf. He was the protector. The provider. He didn't depend on other people. His sister depended on him.

Now he had Callie. And he had the Colters. All of them. It was something he was still getting accustomed to. This whole idea of having a large, extended family. Not just any family, but one that was closely knit and fiercely loyal and would do anything, go to any lengths to protect their own. And he and Lauren were a part of that now.

As he mounted the front steps, he frowned. Usually Callie was at the door to meet him, even if he'd just taken a short trip into town for groceries. He'd grown accustomed to her enthusiastic greetings, and he loved the way she lit up when she saw him again.

He let himself in and opened his mouth to call out to her when he saw her on the couch in the living room. He smiled and put his suitcase down. On quiet feet, he walked to the sofa to stare down at her, curled into a ball, sound asleep.

It wasn't like her to sleep in, but if he had to guess, she'd worked the night before in her brother's bar. He wasn't crazy about her doing it, but he didn't say anything about it. Plus she only did so on the rare occasions when he was out of town and she stayed home.

He leaned down to kiss her temple but as soon as his lips touched her skin, he frowned and drew away.

He put his hand to her forehead, cursing softly when he felt the dry heat radiating from her flesh.

She was sick.

And he'd left her alone.

He knelt by the couch and gently shook her. "Callie. *Dolcezza*, wake up."

She grumbled softly in her sleep, and when she opened her eyes, they were dull. Her cheeks were flushed with fever and she blinked several times as if she were unaware of her surroundings.

Worry ate at his gut. She was his. Completely and utterly his. To love, to protect, and he'd left her alone because he'd been gutted by his sister's plea for help. He should never have left Callie. She should have been with him every step of the way.

"Max," she whispered. Then she smiled. A warm beautiful smile that made the very heart of him ache. "You're home."

He leaned forward to kiss her forehead. "Why didn't you call me? I would have come home immediately. How long have you been sick?"

"Just last night," she croaked. She broke off and rubbed her throat.

He frowned again because he didn't like to see her in discomfort. "Hurt?"

She nodded. "I was okay when I went in. Really. But I started feeling bad not long into it. I didn't want to call Dillon. I thought I could make it. I crashed here as soon as I got home."

He stroked a hand over her forehead. "Wait here. I'll go get something for your fever."

She nodded, her eyes already closing again.

He got up and hurried into the kitchen to the cabinet where they kept the medicine. He frowned as he stared at the acetaminophen and ibuprofen. Finally he grabbed the bottle of ibuprofen, filled a glass half full of water, and went back into the living room.

Callie was back into a tight ball, and he could see her shivering from across the room.

He set the glass on the coffee table and carefully pulled her up and into his arms. She promptly burrowed into his chest and sighed in contentment.

"Take your medicine, *dolcezza*. It will make you feel better. After you've swallowed your pills, I'll take you to bed. I'm sure you'll be more comfortable out of these clothes."

She shook her head against his chest. "Will you build a fire instead? Want to stay here and snuggle."

He kissed the top of her head. "You know I'd do anything to make you feel better."

"Love you."

The soft words came out a little breathy, but they gave him the same thrill they always did. No matter how often she told him, he soaked the words in and held them close. She was everything to him. Her love was the most precious gift he'd ever been given.

"I love you too."

"Missed you."

"I missed you too, *dolcezza*. Now take your medicine so I can build a fire and make you more comfortable. Want your pj's or one of my shirts?"

"Mmm, your shirt, please."

He smiled. It was a wonder he had any sort of a wardrobe left, because she routinely stole his shirts to sleep or lounge in. It gave him a ridiculous thrill to see his clothing on her. Just another stamp of his possession. Like the bands she wore on her wrists. She was his.

Oh, she had a wedding ring. A gorgeous princess-cut diamond that had appalled her with how much it cost. But the platinum cuffs she wore around both wrists . . . Those were more special than even the symbol she wore on her finger. They were what signified her bond to him. Her submission.

They were intricately designed, made especially for her, and he'd had them engraved. On the outside of one, along the bottom, read *two halves of a whole*. And on the other was *we are one*. And on the inside of each in flowing script, *Max and Callie*.

He gently placed the pills on her tongue, then held up the glass so she could sip at the water. She winced and swallowed hard, putting her hand to her throat as the pills finally went down.

"I should take you to the doctor," he said. "You might have strep throat."

"If I'm not better by tomorrow, I'll go. Promise. Going to the doctor means having to move, and right now I just want you to hold me."

He eased her back onto the couch, pressing another kiss to her temple. "I'll be right back. Just need to get some wood to start the fire. I'll get one of my shirts and pillows and another blanket."

She opened her eyes to stare up at him. "I'm so glad you're home."

His heart softened at the love in her eyes and voice. He touched her cheek and then hurried toward the door leading outside to the patio where he kept wood stacked.

A few minutes later, flames licked over the dry wood. He hurriedly collected the items from the bedroom and returned to Callie.

He sat her up and she leaned into him as he undressed her down to her socks. He left them on, not wanting her to get cold, and then pulled his shirt on her and buttoned it all the way to the top.

After kicking off his shoes, he settled onto the couch, propping pillows around her before pulling her against him.

She let out a sigh and snuggled deeply into his arms, burrowing until she was damn near underneath him.

"I feel better already," she said against his chest.

He kissed her again, unable to stop himself from touching her. His arms were full of the woman he loved. He was home. There was no better feeling.

"Is Lauren all right?"

He blew out a long sigh and clutched her a little closer to ease the pain that had suddenly crept through his chest. "No. She's not."

Callie tried to raise her head, but he pulled her down, holding her against him.

"What happened?"

"The man she was with . . ." He couldn't even form the words. It made him angry to even think it. He closed his eyes and rested his cheek against the top of Callie's head. "He abused her."

Such a simple word that in no way conveyed what

this man had done to his baby sister. He'd savaged her. Broken her in body and spirit. Abused? No, the word simply didn't do justice to the damage he'd inflicted.

"Oh, Max, I'm so sorry. What happened? Where is she now? Why didn't you bring her back with you?"

"I tried. She wouldn't come. She's ashamed. God, Callie, I can see it in her eyes. She can barely even look me in the face. She called me only because it had gotten bad, and she was afraid he'd *kill* her. She was hiding at a friend's house, terrified that at any moment the bastard would find her."

This time Callie did sit up and fire was in her eyes. "Max, she has to come here. She shouldn't be alone now!"

"No of course not," he soothed. "I'd never leave her alone and unprotected. I've taken care of it. And yes, I agree. She needs to be here. I don't plan to back off, but she's overwhelmed right now. I was . . ." He broke off and sighed. "I was afraid to push her too hard. She seems so fragile and so near her breaking point. I moved her into an apartment. I've hired someone to shadow her at all times. I also reported the asshole who abused her to the police. There's a warrant out for his arrest right now."

"What did he do to her?" Callie asked, tears brimming in her eyes.

"He beat the hell out of her," Max said, bleakness nearly overwhelming him.. "She says he didn't rape her, but I'm not sure I believe that. I'm so angry. And I feel helpless. She was *ashamed* to call me and wouldn't have if it hadn't been a last resort."

"She'll be safe here," Callie vowed.

Max nodded. "I want her here by Christmas. I'm giving her space and time for the bruises to fade. She didn't want anyone to see her as she is now. It's frustrating because I don't care. I just want her here, with me, where I know she's safe and taken care of. But she refused to even consider coming right now, and as I said, I was afraid to push too hard. I have a cop friend who's going to check in on her as well, and he'll also keep me posted when they find that little bastard."

Callie hugged him tightly and he shook his head at the idea that as sick as she was, she was offering him comfort. He kissed her again and hugged her back, letting her sweetness wash over him.

"I should have seen it." He let some of the pent-up despair that had lived with him for the last few days ease from his chest. Grief was thick in his throat. "I've always checked up on her boyfriends in the past. But this time I let it go. I told myself she wasn't a baby anymore. That I should trust her judgment."

Callie reached up and cupped his face. She looked at him with such love and tenderness that, again, he was shamed by the thought that he should be doing all he could to offer *her* comfort.

"What could you have done?" she asked softly. "You can't live her life for her, Max. She has to make her own choices. How could you have known? Men who abuse women don't wear a sign. A lot of the time they're outwardly charming. Nice guys. No one would ever guess what they do behind closed doors."

"It just makes me sick to see her the way she is now. She's so sweet. Sees the best in everyone. And now she's full of shame for something that was done to her."

"She'll get it back. She'll come here. We'll surround her with love and support and she'll get her confidence back. I don't know that you've ever heard the details of how my mom met my dads, but she was abused by her first husband. She knows what it's like. She'll take Lauren in and mother her senseless, and my dads will kick the ass of anyone who comes near her."

Max smiled. "She loves your family. I think she's awed by them."

"You have to go get her, Max," Callie urged. "Soon."

He pulled her to him and stroked his hand down her back. "I will, *dolcezza*. I will. But first, I'm going to get you well again. I'm not leaving you when you're so sick."

CHAPTER 3

WARM lips nuzzled her neck, sending chill bumps dancing down her spine. Holly Colter smiled and turned into her husband's arms.

"Good morning," Adam murmured just before he captured her lips in a long, tender kiss.

She sighed because this never got old. It was the way he'd greeted her every morning for more than thirty years. She returned his kiss hungrily even as she melted more firmly into his strong embrace.

"I love you."

He pulled away and smiled. "Love you too, baby."

They both turned when they heard the back door

into the kitchen open. Ethan and Ryan came in, stomping snow from their boots. Her heart melted as their gazes found hers, as if they'd looked immediately for her.

"Is it still snowing?" she asked.

Ethan nodded. "Not too bad. Just steady. Supposed to quit by this afternoon."

She broke away from Adam and closed the distance between them. Ryan caught her first, pulling her into his arms. His face was cold, his lips colder, but as soon as their mouths met, heat surged through her veins.

He slipped his hand into her hair and curled his fingers around the strands, holding her in place as he devoured her lips.

As soon as he relinquished his hold on her, Ethan tugged her toward him. He kissed her but dropped his mouth down to nuzzle at her neck.

"Are the roads clear?" she asked as Ethan tucked her into his side.

Adam frowned. "I think so. Why do you ask?"

Holly rolled her eyes because she knew what was coming. But she barged ahead anyway. Her men hadn't changed one iota over the years. She didn't love them any less but it didn't mean she paid them any mind when they started in with their worrying.

"I'm going to see Lily. Thought I'd call Callie and see if she wanted to ride over with me."

"Max is back," Ryan said. "I saw his SUV before we came in. Doubt we'll see Callie for at least a day."

Holly chuckled softly. She was glad Max was back home. Callie had missed him fiercely. She was always glad when her family was where they belonged. Home. On their mountain. Right where she could see them and talk to them anytime she wanted.

"Guess I'll be going to Lily's by myself then."

Adam's frown grew bigger and he shook his head. "You know one of us will drive you over."

"Not necessary," she said lightly. "Lily and I have women stuff to do and you'll just get in the way."

Ryan scowled but he didn't argue.

"Take the SUV and make sure it's in four-wheel drive," Ethan said.

Holly sighed. "At what point will I be able to get into a vehicle to drive myself into town without the three of you worrying?"

Adam sent her a quelling stare. "Try never? We'll always worry when you aren't with us, baby. That ain't going to change. And it's not like you're taking a drive down some city street or the interstate. The drive down the mountain is dangerous even in great weather. It's snowing and the roads are wet and messy."

She broke from Ethan, went over to Adam, and stood up on tiptoe to brush her lips over his. "I'll be fine. Do any of you need anything from town?"

They all shook their heads.

"Call one of us when you get there," Ethan said.

She sent him an exasperated look.

"Just do it," Ryan growled.

She left the room, grumbling under her breath, but as soon as she was away, she broke into a huge smile. Her heart felt as light as it had so many years ago. The love of her husbands was constant. It was true. It was her shelter.

LILY drove aimlessly, her direction unclear. The wipers moved across her windshield, melting the spiraling snowflakes in a wet path across the glass.

Instinctively she turned toward home and the road at the edge of town that led upward to the cabin where she lived with Seth, Michael, and Dillon.

When she pulled into the drive, she parked and sat for a long moment before opening the door. A whoosh of cold air skittered over her. She shivered but plunged out into the chill, needing something to center her.

She dragged her sweater around her and trudged through the snow toward the back of the house where her husbands had built a private memorial to Rose. It had been a gift to her, a place where she could go and be at peace, surrounded by the mountains and the quiet.

The rose of Sharon vine that covered a trellis framing a spectacular vista was brown and withered, the burst of color long gone since winter had descended on the mountains.

She perched on the edge of a wooden bench that Dillon had crafted with his own hands. Intricately carved on the seat was a flowering vine mirroring the one on the trellis. Roses for Rose.

Tears crowded her vision as she looked up. She inhaled deeply, taking in the cold, crisp air. Snowflakes landed on her lashes and she blinked them, and her tears, away.

But they continued, warm trails down her cheeks, quickly turning to ice.

"I don't know what to do," she whispered. "Help me."

Her chest swelled with grief and sadness. And fear. So much fear that it threatened to overwhelm her.

"I don't know if I can do this. I know I was angry with you for taking her from me. I don't deserve your mercy or understanding, but I need your help."

She wiped ineffectually at the tears that ran in streams down her cheeks. Emotion knotted thick in her throat until breathing was nearly impossible.

Losing Rose had nearly destroyed her. She would still be so very lost if it weren't for Seth and his brothers. Seth had taken a young woman from the streets and given her so much love. A family. To her bewilderment, his two brothers had loved her as much as Seth had. There were times she still couldn't wrap her mind around the dynamics of her relationship with the Colter brothers, but she gave thanks for them every single day.

They'd saved her. Given her a reason to live again. They'd given back to her when everything in the world had been cruelly yanked from her.

They'd given her the strength to confront her past. To go to Charles, her former husband, stand up for herself, and tell him he'd been wrong to blame her for their baby daughter's death.

But nothing could give her back her baby.

And now she was pregnant. Another child. A precious gift.

What if she lost it as well?

It wasn't that she didn't trust her husbands. They'd promised her that if and when she was ready to ever have another child, they'd be with her every step of the way and she'd never have to shoulder the burden alone.

But what if it happened anyway?

Sudden infant death syndrome.

Just thinking the words paralyzed her.

How would she be able to sleep for fear of having her baby snatched away in the space of a stolen moment of rest?

"I don't know what to do," she whispered again.

She closed her eyes and bowed her head, whispering the first tentative words of a prayer she'd gone long without saying.

Warmth slid over her as the sun peeked from the thick cover of puffy gray clouds. She opened her eyes and lifted her head as a single ray slipped over her, warming her skin, a barrier to the cold.

The wind picked up and the trees rustled and swayed. The scent of pine was strong and the breeze dried the wetness on her cheeks.

It will be all right.

She imagined the nearly silent whisper that sounded as if it was carried through the trees from the valley. But it comforted her, still.

She hunched forward and carefully put a hand over her still-flat abdomen.

A life.

A tiny, defenseless life lay nestled there underneath her fingers. Already precious. And loved. Loved so very much.

She hugged herself and rocked back and forth, willing the fear to dissipate. She was strong. So much stronger than before.

But no matter how strong she was now, she wouldn't survive another loss.

The peal of her cell phone disturbed the peaceful solitude. She jumped and then reached into her pocket for the phone. It was her mother-in-law's ringtone and Lily's pulse ratcheted up.

Someone had probably seen her at the doctor's, and Holly was likely calling to see if everything was okay. Lily wasn't ready to divulge such unsettling news. She needed time to come to terms with her pregnancy before she blurted it out to her family.

Family.

She closed her eyes, wrapping herself in the comfort and knowledge that she had the best family in the entire world. They loved her and she loved them dearly.

With shaking fingers, she hit the button to receive the call and put the phone to her ear.

"Hello?"

"Lily, dear, it's Holly. How are you?"

"F-fine. I'm fine. How are you?"

"I'm on my way over, actually. I hope you're home! I didn't even think to call before I left. You know how I am. Once I get an idea in my head, I act. And to be honest, I was more focused on being able to get past the husbands without the third degree. You know how they are about me driving myself into town."

Lily smiled, picturing Holly rolling her eyes as she always did when she talked about the three older Colter men.

"Yes, I'm home."

"Oh good," Holly breathed. "I have a huge favor to ask."

Lily let a sigh of relief. Her mother-in-law wasn't calling because she knew Lily had been to the doctor.

She stood rapidly, still holding the phone as she headed toward the back door. It wouldn't do for Holly to see the mess Lily was in. She'd latch on and there'd be no avoiding the issue.

She wiped frantically at her face even as she murmured a good-bye to Holly. She tossed the phone onto the counter and then headed into the bathroom.

She had about fifteen minutes to make it look like her world hadn't just been tilted on its axis.

CHAPTER 4

LILY smiled broadly at herself in the mirror. She grimaced and then let her lips fall. The smile looked exactly the way it felt—fake and forced. When the doorbell rang, she sighed and turned away.

Makeup did wonders, though Lily didn't normally wear much—and she didn't have much on now. Just enough to disguise the signs of grief that had ravaged her face earlier.

She hurried to the door, putting on a genuine, warm smile before opening it.

Holly bustled in from the cold, immediately pulling Lily into a huge hug. Holly wasn't a large woman by any stretch, but she hugged like a bear. Lily felt it to her soul and closed her eyes as her mother-in-law soothed and patted and made Lily feel like she was bathed in sunshine.

"Are none of those boys of mine home today?" Holly asked when she finally released Lily.

Lily shut the door, took Holly's coat, and shook her head. "Dillon went in early because Callie was working the bar last night. He never likes it when she does and neither does Max. Max called, wanting him to at least make sure she didn't sleep on the couch in the office, so I'm sure he went in and made her go home."

"Ah," Holly said. "Well, Max is home so he'll take care of that, I suppose."

"I'm so glad they'll be here this Christmas."

Holly's entire face lit up. "Oh yes, me too. My whole family here for Christmas. I'm so excited, I can't stand it."

As they entered the living room, Lily paused and turned to see Holly staring intently at her.

"Are you all right, Lily? You look a little pale."

Lily swallowed and forced a brighter smile. "I'm fine."

Holly frowned but didn't pursue the matter, and

now Lily worried that she'd mention her concerns to her sons. Impulsively, she reached for Holly's hand and squeezed, feeling better for the contact.

"Holly, I'm fine. Now tell me what favor you need. You know I'd do anything for you."

Her mother-in-law turned, took both of Lily's hands in hers, her eyes dancing with excitement. "I want you to teach me how to cook."

Lily's mouth dropped open. Of all the things that Holly could have said, this was the farthest thing from Lily's mind. She stared at Holly for several long seconds before she finally found her tongue.

"What on earth for?"

Holly sighed, let go of Lily's hands, and then settled on the couch. Lily took a seat next to her, tucking one leg underneath her and rotating so they faced each other.

"It's been a running family joke for years that I can't cook and that my husbands have always provided the meals for our family—which is totally true, mind you. It's never bothered me, but this year . . . This Christmas I'd like to put the food on the table for my family and know that I made it. I want this year to be special. So much has changed in our family in a short amount of time, and for the first time in a long time we're all going to be together. Last year, Max and Callie spent Christmas overseas. But this year all my babies will be at home where they belong."

Lily leaned over to put her arm around Holly. She squeezed and then smiled. "Of course I'll help. When I'm done, you'll be able to prepare the best holiday meal the Colters have ever tasted."

Holly beamed and then threw her arms around Lily, hugging her tight. "I knew I could count on you. Now, where do we start?"

Holly's bright enthusiasm was a balm to Lily's soul. Some of her fear and melancholy lifted away as she focused on a way to make her mother-in-law happy.

"Well, it depends on what you'd like to serve. Are we going traditional with a bird, dressing, and the fixings? Or do you want to go for wow factor?"

Holly pulled away, a pensive frown on her face. "I kind of like wow, but maybe that's too much to expect in such a short amount of time."

"Oh, I don't know. What if we did something creole?"

"Oh yum. There's a Cajun restaurant in Denver that I love. The husbands take me there when we're in the city."

"Hmm, okay. How does a pan-seared catfish fillet covered with crawfish étouffée sound?"

"Like my mouth is watering!"

Lily grinned. Holly's excitement was infectious. "For starters, we could do a lobster bisque and crawfish-stuffed shrimp. I have an awesome recipe for homemade rolls that won't take any time in the bread machine. Then we'll have the fish and étouffée as the main course. For dessert, I'm thinking caramel Heath bar pie."

"Has anyone ever told you what a culinary genius you are? Dillon has always been the master chef in the family but you, my dear, he can't hold a candle to."

"Oh, I love it when you stroke my ego. I'll love getting to take credit for getting Mama Colter to create a perfect meal. Dillon will be bitter forever. He keeps swearing he's going to get you into the kitchen."

Holly snorted. "Dillon and I would never make it together. I'd murder my own child before it was over with."

Lily rose. "Well then, let's go shopping. We have groceries to buy and a kitchen to mess up. We're on a tight timeline here. We only have until the guys get home from work, and if they catch us in the kitchen or see the kitchen in a mess, they'll want to know what on earth we're up to."

Holly shot to her feet, an excited smile lighting up her face. "Thank you, Lily. I can't wait!"

"You'll have to find a way to get over here every day until we get this right," Lily cautioned. "You'll have to think of something to say to the dads so they don't get suspicious."

"Oh, I'll handle them," Holly said airily, mischief sparkling in her eyes. "Tomorrow is Saturday so I'll come over in the morning and make the boys go over to their fathers'."

CALLIE stirred, tried to swallow, and grimaced. She opened her eyes to see Max staring intently down at her, his lips set in a fine line.

"Your throat hurting worse?"

She nodded. "Need something to drink."

He leaned forward, holding her tightly so she didn't slide from his lap, and retrieved the glass of water sitting on the coffee table.

She drank greedily, trying not to flinch at the discomfort it caused her throat. Her fever had broken and she was damp with sweat. Where before she'd been freezing and sure she'd never get warm again, now she was hot, aching, and twitchy all over.

When she was done drinking, she lay limply on Max's chest, her eyes closed in exhaustion. It was ridiculous really. There was no reason for her to feel so weak, but she couldn't do battle with a kitten at the moment.

The doorbell rang and she groaned, but Max simply lifted her to the side and settled her among the pillows. As if he was expecting someone. She glanced up, her suspicions confirmed when Max opened the door and Dr. Burton came in, shaking snow from his hat before Max took it and his coat from him.

She huffed in exasperation as Max and the doctor returned to the couch. "Max, really. This was so unnecessary. I can't believe you made Dr. Burton come all this way. What about his patients?"

"You *are* my patient, missy," Dr. Burton said in reprimand. "You should have come to see me first thing this morning instead of crawling home to suffer alone."

Callie allowed him to poke and prod at her. He looked at her throat, made several noncommittal noises, and then took out his cell phone.

"Looks like strep to me. Of course, I can't do a test here, but that throat looks bad and, regardless, you need an antibiotic, so we're going on the assumption you have strep. Start the antibiotics immediately and by tomorrow afternoon you should start feeling better."

While Dr. Burton phoned in the prescriptions, Max left the room for a moment. Callie snuggled back into the pillows, already feeling the chill returning. A few minutes later, Max came back and spoke to Dr. Burton briefly before showing the other man out.

The next thing Callie knew, Max was back, holding more ibuprofen in his hand.

"Take these, *dolcezza*. Your fever is returning."

She swallowed them down and then sighed in contentment when he sat beside her and pulled her back into his arms.

Then she frowned. "How am I supposed to get the antibiotics?" Obviously Max would have to go into town to get the prescription filled, but the selfish part of her whined at the idea of him leaving.

"I called your mother. Well, actually I called your dads first and they said your mom was in town with Lily, so I then called your mom and asked her to pick up your medicine on her way back. She'll be by in a little while to see you."

"Mom's awesome," Callie croaked out.

Max smiled tenderly down at her. "Moms are the very best when you're sick."

She wasn't so absorbed in her own misery that she'd forgotten Lauren. She'd thought of her all afternoon. Lauren was sweet and shy, so different from Max's dominating personality. It sickened Callie that Lauren had been abused by some asshole she'd trusted.

"Max?"

He swept his hand over her hair, smoothing it from her forehead so he could see her eyes.

"I know you wanted to give Lauren time, but I really think we should go get her."

"You're sick, Callie. I don't think you should be going anywhere."

"You heard the doctor. If I start on antibiotics today, by tomorrow afternoon I'll be feeling better. We could leave for Denver in the morning, take an afternoon flight, and be in New York by tomorrow night. We could be back home with Lauren by the day after tomorrow, and you and I would both feel better."

Max sighed and she knew he was close to caving. His thoughts had been consumed with his sister. Callie knew it, and that he was deeply worried. He was torn between the thought that Callie needed him here and that his sister was wounded, frightened, and alone.

Callie sat up and touched Max's cheek. "I'll be fine, Max. Lauren is more important than some stupid bug I've caught. I know I won't feel better until she's here with us where we both know she's safe, and if I'm that adamant, I can't even imagine how you're feeling. I know you wanted to be gentle and considerate with her, but now isn't the time for that. I vote we go in and don't come back without her."

Max smiled then and pressed his lips to her forehead. "That's what I love most about you, *dolcezza*. You're frighteningly fierce when you set your mind to something. You'd make most men tremble in their boots."

"So we'll do it?"

"Yes. Provided you start your antibiotics immediately and you don't worsen overnight. I'll arrange for my jet to arrive in Denver in the morning, refuel, and be on standby when we get to the airport in the afternoon."

"You're doing the right thing, Max. She needs to

be surrounded by people who love her right now even if she thinks she wants to be alone."

He stroked his hand through her hair, idly fingering the strands. "I just want my sister back. The woman I saw a few days ago isn't the sister I remember. She's changed so much just since I saw her last."

His fingers tightened in her hair and his expression grew darker. "I hate that bastard for what he did. Not just for the physical damage he did, but because he crushed her spirit. She's a shadow of her former self, and I guess my fear is that she won't get that spirit back."

"She will. She just needs time. My dads and brothers will baby her, as will you. She'll see that all men aren't bastards. In time she'll trust herself again."

"You're right, of course. Now, for a time, let's focus on you. Are you hungry? Would you like some hot tea for your throat? Tell me what it is you want and I'll make it happen."

"Oh, Max, you should know better than to give me that much leeway," she teased.

"On the contrary," he murmured. "I mean every word. You're my life. Your happiness and well-being are everything to me. I don't like to see you not feeling well. Now, are you hungry?"

They were interrupted by the peal of Max's cell phone. Unlike her, he didn't have a ringtone for everyone. It drove her crazy because she liked to know who was calling even before she looked at the display screen.

He put the phone to his ear. "Hello, Mrs. C."

Callie smiled at the mention of her mother.

"No, actually we were just discussing whether she was hungry. Hang on. I'll ask."

He put the phone to his shoulder and turned to Callie. "Your mom wants to know if you'd like some of Lily's chicken noodle soup."

Callie's mouth instantly watered. "Oh my God, yes. Please."

Max chuckled and picked the phone back up. "That's a yes. All right. Be careful and we'll see you soon."

He put the phone back down. "She's on her way. She's swinging by to pick up your medicine and then she'll be up."

Thirty minutes later, Holly breezed through the door without knocking and shooed Max back when he started to rise. She set the container of soup on the coffee table, then bent over to give Max a hug and a kiss.

She perched on the edge of the couch and enfolded

Callie in her arms. "Sorry you're sick, baby. I brought your medicine and some of Lily's soup. You should be feeling better in no time with Max here to take care of you."

Callie smiled and snuggled into her mother's embrace. No matter how old she got, she'd never be too old for her mother to baby. There just wasn't anything better than a mother's hug and unconditional love. She sighed and squeezed before finally relinquishing her grip on her mom.

Then she glanced back at Max, her gaze questioning. Slowly he nodded, understanding what she was asking.

"Mom, Max and I are going to New York tomorrow to bring Lauren home."

Holly's brows came together. "But you're sick. Maybe Max should go. You could stay with me and your dads, or if you prefer, I'll come stay here with you."

Callie shook her head and then put her hand over her mother's. "Mom, she's been abused. The guy she was with . . . He hurt her terribly. She didn't want to come back with Max, but I think if I go back with him, together we can convince her to return here. She needs to be surrounded by people who love her."

Holly's eyes were stricken, and then anger lit fire in their depths. Her fingers curled around Callie's hand and tightened. "Bring her home. We'll take care of her and we'll kick the ass of anyone who ever tries to hurt her again."

Max smiled and leaned forward to kiss his mother-in-law on the cheek. "I can see now where Callie gets her ferocity. You, Mama Colter, are the best, and Lauren and I are lucky to have been swept into your fold."

Holly dug into the bag she'd tossed down beside the soup and shook out one of the antibiotic pills. "Here, baby. Take your medicine so you can get to feeling better. Now that everyone will be home, we've got Christmas to hold, and we're going to make the most of it."

CHAPTER 5

SOMETHING was bothering Lily. Seth watched her from the doorway of her studio as she tugged at her bottom lip with her teeth. She dabbed paint with her brush, but he could see the distant look in her eyes that told him she wasn't really focusing on her painting.

She'd been quiet and distracted for a few days now, and it was driving Seth—and his brothers—crazy.

Lily wasn't much of a complainer and she rarely bothered to volunteer information when something was wrong. Seth, Michael, and Dillon usually had to drag it out of her.

They'd actually been delighted once when they'd managed to piss her off enough that she'd lit into them with both barrels. His ears still stung from the dressing-down she'd given them, but they'd grinned the entire time she was doing it until she'd realized they were smiling, and then she'd given them bewildered looks and demanded to know what was so funny.

Seth had pulled her into his arms, peppered her beautiful face with kisses, and then explained to her that it was okay to unload on them. About anything at all. No matter how insignificant she thought it was. That was what they were here for. To be her rock. To protect her. To love her. Always.

He still marveled at the miracle she was. At how content he and his brothers were. She'd given them so much and they were just as determined to give back to her.

Dillon appeared at the doorway and frowned when he saw Seth staring in at Lily. "Mom's here to see Lily and we've been banished to go watch football with the dads. I smell a rat."

Seth stared pensively at Lily as she looked up when she heard them talking. A soft smile removed the consternation that had been evident moments before.

"You're staring."

Seth relaxed, unable to remain thoughtful when her smile tugged at his heartstrings. "Is it a crime to stare at a beautiful woman?"

She shook her head but her cheeks darkened with a hint of color. No matter how often they told her she was beautiful, that she was their world, she always got shy when they gave her compliments.

"Mom's here. She's kicking us out. Know anything about that?"

Lily's eyebrow arched. "What, she can't come to visit me without you getting suspicious?"

Dillon snorted. "I don't trust my mother when she's smiling that sweetly at me. She patted me on the cheek and called me her baby. I know she's up to something."

Seth snorted at the image of their petite mother patting Mr. Badass on the cheek and cooing at him. "Mama's boy," he taunted.

Dillon flashed a grin. "Yeah, so? You're just mad because she loves me better."

Seth rolled his eyes and then Lily laughed. God, he loved that sound. She had the most beautiful laughter. It was a far cry from the sad-eyed woman he'd first seen in the line at a soup kitchen for the homeless.

She'd been so somber and serious then. That she laughed and smiled so readily now made his chest tighten.

Lily got up and walked to him, sliding her arm around his waist even as he pulled her into his side. He kissed the mop of dark curls and rubbed his cheek over the top of her head.

"Come on. We don't want to keep Mom waiting."

Lily slid her hand into Dillon's and tugged him along behind her and Seth as they made their way into the living room. They both were warm and vibrant against her. Strength. Comfort. Her entire world.

And there was Michael, sitting with his mom, but as soon as she and his brothers entered the room, his gaze found hers and was so full of love that her heart stuttered.

There was so much love in this family. That she'd found a place here in their midst still boggled her mind.

She belonged. This was hers. They belonged to her.

It would be all right. She just had to keep telling herself that.

"Lily!" Holly exclaimed as she rose. "I hope I didn't disturb your painting."

Lily accepted her mother-in-law's warm hug and returned the embrace with one of her own.

"You're never a bother. I'm glad you're here. Do you know if Callie is feeling better?"

She marveled at just how innocent the exchange seemed. She could barely suppress her grin. So far, things had gone off without a hitch. It truly looked as though Holly had popped in for a visit and wanted to spend time with her daughter-in-law.

Holly's expression sobered for a moment. "She and Max are flying to New York this afternoon. They left for Denver this morning."

Dillon scowled. "What the hell? She's sick. She doesn't need to be flying all over the damn country. I knew I shouldn't have let her work the bar while Max was gone. He hates it and so do I."

Holly sighed as Seth and Michael both gave frowns of disapproval as well.

"It was necessary. There are issues with Lauren. Max didn't want Callie to go either, but she insisted, and she was right to do so. Lauren needs them. She needs all of us right now."

Lily's brow furrowed at the sorrow in Holly's voice. "What happened?"

Holly's lips turned down. "She was abused by a man she trusted."

Lily's husbands' frowns turned to deep scowls. If there was one thing the Colter men held true to, it was that women were to be cherished above all things. It was a principle passed from fathers to sons and was evidenced in the way the Colter women were coddled, pampered, and protected.

"Damn," Michael muttered.

It was common knowledge in the family that Holly had escaped an abusive husband many years earlier. It was what had brought her to the Colter men. They'd nearly lost her to the bastard, and the subject of abuse was always bound to make any of the Colter men immediately snarly.

Holly stared at each of her boys in turn, love warming her eyes. "She'll need us all. We're her family now. All she has left is Max. Max said she's ashamed and doesn't want anyone to see her or know what's happened. I'm counting on you boys to spoil her rotten and make her feel at home."

"You know we will, Mom," Dillon said, his face still dark with a frown. "Damn it, but that sucks. She's a little bit of a thing."

Lily nodded her agreement, wincing at the image

of some man knocking Lauren around. They'd all met Lauren only once—at Callie and Max's wedding—and she'd been a beautiful, shy young woman, so different from Max's overpowering presence and quiet confidence.

Michael's arm came around Lily, and he pulled her into his side. He squeezed almost as if he knew how much she needed his comfort and support. And oh God, she did. More than anything she needed to know that everything would be all right. That he and his brothers would be right here, with her. Always.

"When will they be back?" Seth asked quietly.

Holly shrugged. "I'm not sure. You know how your sister is when she sets her mind to something. She won't be coming home without Lauren and it won't matter what Lauren thinks she wants."

Michael chuckled. "Takes after Dillon. Both stubborn hardheads."

Dillon curled his lip at his brother.

Holly rolled her eyes. "Okay boys, time to clear out."

Michael's eyes narrowed in suspicion. "I don't trust you."

Holly lifted both eyebrows in mock dismay. "What a thing to say to your mother! Go on now. All of you shoo. Your fathers are expecting you."

"It's sad that even when I'm thirty-three years old, my mother can still make me feel ten," Seth grumbled as he got his coat out of the closet.

He tossed jackets to Michael and Dillon, then headed back toward Lily.

Without a word, he hugged her up tight and squeezed until she was breathless. Then he kissed her, his hand lingering on her cheek.

"Be back later, baby."

Lily kissed Dillon and Michael and watched as they shuffled out the door. Then she turned to her mother-in-law. "Ready to get to work?"

CHAPTER 6

"THIS is ridiculous," Max muttered as he drove down the interstate. "I never should have let you talk me into this."

Callie huddled in the blanket Max had wrapped around her and adjusted the heater vent to hit her more squarely.

"I just took some more ibuprofen. My fever will break soon," she said, trying to control her chattering teeth.

"You can barely talk," Max said. "And your throat hurts. You have chills and fever and you have no business getting on a plane. I should check you into a hotel and have your dads or brothers come get you."

"Don't you dare," Callie growled. "I can lie down on your plane same as I can lie down at home in my bed. What's the difference?"

"The difference is you'd have someone to fuss over you, you'd have a more comfortable bed, and you wouldn't be out in the cold and snow."

She made a disgruntled sound and burrowed deeper into her blanket. "Lauren needs us both. I can use my sickness as a trump card. If she starts arguing, I'll feign weakness and be pitiful. Then she'll have to come so you can whisk me back home to my sickbed."

Max shook his head. "You're diabolical."

She grinned around her quivering lips. "You love that about me."

He shot her an amused look. "I love you more when that evil streak isn't aimed at me."

For a moment she stared at him, suddenly struck, as she was so often, by how much she adored this man. Was he perfect? Oh hell no. He'd made his fair share of mistakes. But he'd done everything in his power to make up for those mistakes. He showed her every day how much he loved and adored her. He took care of her. He showered her with affection. She was one spoiled woman and she loved every minute of it.

"Do I even want to know what you're thinking?" he asked with a resigned sigh.

"I love you," she said softly.

His eyes darkened and his fingers tightened around the wheel. "I love you too, *dolcezza*. I give thanks every day that you are able to love me after all we've been through."

She smiled and reached over to lace her fingers through his. He raised her hand to his mouth and pressed a kiss to her palm.

"What's done is done. It does neither of us any good to dwell on the past. Not when our future is so very bright."

Max gripped her hand for a long moment and he swallowed almost as if he wanted to speak but couldn't. When he finally spoke, it was to change the subject entirely.

"Are you comfortable? Perhaps you should sleep for a while. We still have an hour and a half until we get to the airport."

She leaned her head back against the headrest and closed her eyes, willing to let him veer into neutral territory. She knew he still lost sleep when he remembered how close he'd come to losing her. "I think you're right. I feel like a wet noodle. I want to be rested for when we meet Lauren."

"Sleep then, love. I'll wake you when we get to the plane."

DESPITE her protests, Max carried her, wrapped in the blanket from his SUV, onto his jet. He made sure the pilot had warmed the interior and was ready to go the moment they arrived.

Within minutes they took off and Max didn't wait long to unbuckle her and pull her into his arms once more. He carried her back to the lounge area to a comfortable leather couch, and he settled onto it, holding her against his chest.

She dozed for most of the flight. Max woke her up once to give her more medicine when he noted that she was once again shivering and then she drifted back off, snuggled deeply into his embrace.

By the time they landed in New York, some of the bone-deep chill had worn off. Callie felt wrung out, but at least she wasn't so cold she couldn't function. What she needed most now was a bath to wash off all the sweat and the sticky sensation. But she didn't want to delay even a moment in going to get Lauren.

It amused Max that she insisted the pilot remain on standby. They wouldn't be more than a few hours—over her dead body were they going to remain in a city with the asshole loose who'd beaten Lauren.

Even sick, grumpy, having a sore throat, and feeling like complete crap, she was a woman on a mission.

Max whisked her into a waiting car and directed the driver to take them to the apartment where he'd relocated Lauren.

"And you're sure she's okay?" Callie asked anxiously as she watched traffic drive through melting puddles of snow.

Max put his hand over hers. "Relax, *dolcezza*. I get hourly reports from the men I hired to guard her. She goes nowhere without their protection. No one gets into her apartment without their knowledge and consent. She's safe."

She blew out her breath. Yes, if Max had hired someone to protect his sister, he would have hired only the best. Still, she'd feel much better when Lauren was back home with them in the midst of Callie's loving family.

At times like this, a girl needed family above all else. Callie was going to make sure Lauren had it.

Thirty minutes later, they pulled up to an apartment building.

"I don't suppose I can convince you to remain in the car where it's warm and dry while I go collect Lauren," Max said.

Callie shook her head emphatically and Max chuckled.

"I didn't think so. Well, come on then. Let's hurry. I want you back home where I can take better care of you."

Max got out and helped Callie onto the sidewalk before tucking her firmly under his arm. They hurried toward the building, where Max scanned a security card to gain access.

As they headed toward the elevator, Max pulled out his cell phone, punched in a number, and then put the phone to his ear.

"This is Wilder. I'm coming up with my wife."

Max ushered her onto the elevator, suddenly all business. He was tense and his face was set in stone. Already he was preparing for battle. A battle he didn't intend to lose. Callie put her hand on his arm and gently squeezed.

His expression softened and he pulled her closer to him. He brushed a kiss across the top of her head, then squeezed her back.

The elevator opened and they stepped into the hall. When they rounded the corner, they were met by two very broad-shouldered, intimidating men. Callie instinctively stepped closer to Max.

These weren't the polished, suave, security detail–type men in suits she'd expected. They were rough around the edges. Looked mean as hell. Were as big as damn mountains. But the upside? Callie couldn't imagine anyone in their right mind fucking with these two. That included Lauren's loser of an ex-boyfriend.

"How is she?" Max asked in clipped tones.

One of the men scowled. "Hasn't left her apartment since she arrived."

Max swore under his breath. "Has she been eating?"

The second man nodded. "We've made sure of it. She's not too happy with us—or you—at the moment."

Max grimaced, then turned to Callie. "Callie, this is Liam Prescott and Noah Sullivan, the two men I hired to oversee Lauren's safety." He glanced back at the two men. "This is my wife, Callie."

"Ma'am," Liam said as he dipped his head respectfully.

Callie swallowed and continued to stare at the two boulders. Yes, boulders. It was the only word to describe them. They were hard as stone and had muscles in places Callie had never imagined muscles to be.

"She probably hasn't left her apartment because she's scared to death of them," she whispered to Max.

Liam chuckled. "No ma'am, she's not afraid of us. She's pissed. There's a difference. I'd rather have her pissed off than in danger though."

Noah shrugged like it didn't matter to him one way or another.

Callie cleared her throat. "Well, um, we've come to take her home with us. I mean, not that you aren't doing a good job—I'm sure you are—but she belongs with family."

A smile quirked the corner of Liam's mouth. "We don't bite, Mrs. Wilder."

Max silenced him with a glare.

"Let's go, Max," Callie said impatiently.

Max motioned her ahead and Callie gingerly walked by the two mountains and knocked lightly on Lauren's door. A moment later it swung open, and Lauren was there with a disgruntled look on her face.

"I ate, okay?"

Then she stopped and her eyes went wide with surprise. "Callie! What are you . . . I thought it was them . . . Max?"

Callie pulled her petite sister-in-law into a hug and squeezed her fiercely. When she let her go, Max held out his arms and Lauren went into his embrace.

"Are you all right?" he asked her quietly.

She nodded as she pulled away. "Come in. Both of you."

The two mountains took their positions by the door and Lauren closed the door with a sharp bang.

"Pains in my ass," Lauren muttered as she turned away. "Now, what are you two doing here? Not that I'm not thrilled to see you."

Callie studied her sister-in-law closely and didn't like what she saw. Behind the façade of normalcy was an exhausted, shadowed woman with fear in her eyes. Callie's heart ached for her.

There were deep smudges underneath Lauren's eyes, and she looked much thinner than the last time Callie had seen her. Her arms and neck were covered by the long-sleeved shirt and scarf she wore, but Max had told Callie about the dark bruises that marred her skin.

"We came to take you home," Callie said firmly.

Lauren's lips twisted unhappily, but before she could launch a protest, Callie held up a hand to silence her.

"This is not up for discussion. Max and I both agree you need to be with family. My parents are dying to get their hands on you. My brothers will spoil you rotten."

Lauren shook her head but Callie wasn't giving up.

"You need us, Lauren," she said softly. "Everybody needs their family. Especially when something terrible happens. I should know. I shut mine out when I should have been wallowing in all their love and support. Come home with us. I'm not leaving without you."

Max spoke up for the first time. "She's right, baby." His voice was tender and coaxing. "And you know how fierce Callie is when she's set her mind to something. She's sick with strep throat and a hundred-and-four fever but hell if she wasn't getting on a plane to come bring you home."

Lauren smiled faintly. "My brother sounds afraid of you."

Callie grinned. "That's because he's a smart man."

Lauren's expression grew more troubled. "I don't know about this."

Callie took her hands and squeezed. "There's nothing to know or think about. There's nothing for you here. Come home with us and heal. There's no better place to be than surrounded by the Colters."

Tears gathered in Lauren's dark eyes and her lips trembled. Then finally she nodded. "Okay. I'll come."

CHAPTER 7

"I'M starting to get worried," Dillon said bluntly.

He folded his arms over his chest and stared over the bar at his two brothers seated on bar stools. Seth and Michael had come into the pub during their lunch hour on the day the pub was closed.

Usually Dillon would be home. With Lily. Usually if Seth was free for lunch, he came home to be with Lily. If Michael wasn't busy at his practice, he would be with her.

But today, they had agreed to meet at Mountain Pass, away from Lily. To discuss . . . her.

"She's not herself," Dillon continued, eyeing the

unease on his brothers' faces. It was an unease he distinctly shared. Something wasn't right, and it was high time to figure out what the hell it was.

"No," Michael said wearily. "She isn't. She puts on a good front, but when she thinks we aren't looking, she seems . . . sad. Worried."

Seth leaned his forehead against the edges of his palms and blew out a deep breath. "God almighty, I don't know what it could be, but it scares the hell out of me. What if . . . what if this whole thing isn't working for her anymore? What if she isn't happy with the arrangement?"

Seth had voiced the question uppermost in Dillon's mind. He'd pinpointed Dillon's number one worry, and judging by the look on Michael's face, Seth had nailed Michael's primary concern too.

"Shit," Dillon muttered.

Michael shook his head, his lips set into a fine line. "No. That can't be it. It can't. Lily . . ."

"Lily what?" Seth demanded. "Lily's happy? I think we all know that isn't true right now."

"We don't have to assume worst-case scenario," Dillon pointed out.

"Why the fuck are we sitting here talking about worst-case scenarios?" Michael asked in disgust. "We should be asking her what's wrong. This speculating is making me crazy."

"Because we're all afraid of the answer," Seth said quietly.

Dillon blew out his breath. "Yeah. Right there. Scared shitless, and I don't mind admitting it."

"Do you think Mom knows what's up?" Michael asked. "She's been over there a lot lately. I don't know what they're up to. Could be nothing. But Mom doesn't usually come over and kick us out."

"Could be anything," Seth said. "She might be working on a Christmas present for the dads. There are a lot of explanations for why Mom would be coming to see Lily all hush-hush."

Dillon clenched his fist in frustration. "So we're back to square one. Which is that we have no idea what the hell is going on with the woman we love, no idea how to fix it, because again, we have no idea what it is and we're all too chickenshit to ask. Have I got it about right?"

Michael gave a disgusted sigh. "That about sums it up."

"So what do we do?" Dillon asked.

He hated how fucking helpless he felt. Like his entire life was on the line and he had no control over how it turned out. He knew his brothers felt the same because their expressions said it all.

They'd all secretly feared that the relationship wouldn't work out. It was their number one fear.

Though their fathers had a very nontraditional relationship with their mother, it had never occurred to them that they would follow in the same path. It hadn't been discussed. No one had ever suggested it. They'd certainly had relationships, flings, whatever the hell you wanted to call them, with other women, and they damn sure hadn't ever called any of the others up and asked him if he was up for a foursome.

Seth had been the first to make that connection with Lily, but it hadn't meant that his was any more intense than Michael's or even Dillon's own. From the moment Dillon had laid eyes on her, he'd known without a doubt that she was his and that he'd go to any lengths to possess her.

He hadn't cared that Seth had already staked a claim or that she was in town because she'd come with him. There was no way he could walk away from her and settle for a relationship as her brother-in-law. Oh hell no.

It had taken some discussion between the brothers

before they'd realized that they had a huge problem. They were all in love with the same woman and none of them were willing to take a step back.

No one in their family so much as blinked an eye. Hell, no one in the town of Clyde would have been surprised. But Lily?

This wasn't normal to her. It wasn't something she'd been exposed to all her life. They'd come at her like fucking bulldozers.

Maybe now she was having some serious second thoughts. Maybe she didn't like having to juggle three men in a relationship.

It was automatic for Dillon to think back, to try to figure out if he or one of his brothers had been demanding. Expected too much from her. But no, they were always so careful. Because they feared overwhelming her, because they feared pushing her too far.

Fuck it, but this was for the birds. It was time to get their asses home and figure out what the hell was wrong with their woman so they could make it right.

LILY tugged her sweater tighter around her waist as she walked through the small grove of aspens behind the cabin. She loved this trail, especially in fall when the leaves burned gold and were so brilliant to look at that it made her eyes hurt.

She should have taken her heavier coat but she hadn't planned on going this far. She'd only meant to sit awhile on her bench and stare at the vista through Rose's memorial.

It had begun to snow, adding another thin layer to the ground cover that crunched beneath her boots. They weren't due for any heavy snow, at least not today. She hadn't checked the extended forecast to know what lay beyond.

The last several days had been good because Holly had kept Lily busy with teaching her how to cook. But the downside was that Lily was no closer to knowing how to break the news to her husbands because she hadn't had time to think.

She was always around someone. She hadn't had any time alone to just be. To think and consider. To face her fears and resolve to share her secret with the men she loved.

She took her hands out of her pockets and blew on them to warm the tips. She hadn't brought her gloves either, but she wasn't so cold that she was compelled to return to the cabin. Not yet.

There was a point she wanted to reach, where she

could look out and see forever. Over the valley and down the ridge. The most beautiful country she'd ever seen.

This was her home. She had to constantly remind herself that it was hers. She had a place in the world.

And now so would her child.

She paused, taking that last step, and then rested her hand on the trunk of an aspen as she peered out, taking in the breathtaking view.

After a moment, she leaned her back against the tree and soaked in her surroundings. The crisp, clean smell of the air. The scent of pine. The tickle of snow-flakes as they drifted lazily down, melting on her cheeks.

Her breath came out in a fog, and after a while, her breathing slowed and evened out. For the last few days, she'd existed in denial. She hadn't allowed herself to think about the baby, much less dwell on the details. Boy. Girl. Who would it look like?

She'd busied herself with Holly and immersed herself in family, putting on a brave front, not allowing them to see her worry or fear.

But it hadn't helped. She had decisions to make. She had fears to face. All she had to do was reach out and ask for help. Seth, Michael, and Dillon loved her.

She had no doubts there. They'd do anything in the world to make her happy, and they'd help her work through her conflicting emotions about her pregnancy.

She just had to muster the nerve to blurt it all out.

With a resigned sigh, she pushed off the tree and started retracing her steps back to the cabin.

As she drew nearer, she frowned. She could swear she heard her name.

She quickened her step through the aspens but stopped when she heard the distinctive call. It was Seth and he was yelling her name.

Worried that something was wrong, she jogged through the snow, taking care not to slip as she headed down the incline.

She came to an abrupt halt when she broke into the clearing and saw all three of her husbands spread out behind the cabin, obviously looking . . . for her.

CHAPTER 8

MICHAEL was the first to see her. He turned, did a double take, and then charged toward her, calling to his brothers the entire way.

Lily's breath caught in her throat and her pulse accelerated wildly. There was fierce determination—and worry—in her husbands' gazes and she knew that no matter whether she was prepared or not, the time had come. There was no way around it.

Michael ran up to her, took her arms in his hands. "Lily! What on earth are you doing up here? We were worried sick. You aren't even dressed for the cold."

Even as the questions poured out, he pulled her into

his side, wrapping as much of his coat around her as he could while providing her with his body warmth.

His worried gaze cut to his brothers as they ran up, snow kicking up from their boots.

Dillon stood back a little hesitant. "Lily?"

She sent him a reassuring smile. "I'm fine, Dillon. I just went for a walk through the aspen grove. It's such a beautiful day."

Seth frowned. "You aren't dressed to be out tromping around in the snow. You don't even have a coat or gloves."

She shrugged. "I hadn't planned on going that far. I went to sit out on the bench and got the urge to take a walk. I was just heading back. I haven't been out that long."

"Well, let's get you back inside," Michael said. He propelled her toward the house, still holding her tightly against his side.

With a sigh she settled against him, letting his solid strength seep into her body. She leaned her head against his chest and blinked away the snowflakes trapped on her eyelashes.

It was, as she'd said, a truly magnificent day. She loved winter on her mountain. She loved the cabin that Dillon had built himself and later added on to when it had been decided that they would all live here.

Now she looked at it with different eyes. Holly and the dads' cabin . . . it was where all the Colter children had grown up. There was a strong sense of home there. You couldn't walk into their house without being swamped by love. History. The sense of family. There were pictures everywhere. Of Seth, Michael, and Dillon, and then Callie, who'd come along later and had been a surprise.

That house was a symbol of everything she wanted most in the world. She'd always been a little awed by it. The family gatherings on the weekends for dinner. The easy way the Colters demonstrated their love for one another.

She wanted all of that for herself. She wanted to start a new chapter in a solid legacy. She wanted *her* home to be filled with love and laughter. Children. Oh God, children.

Did she have the courage to face her worst fears?

When they got to the house, they filed through the back door. Dillon bent to take off her boots while Seth took her sweater after Michael unwrapped her from his coat.

She headed for the kitchen, thinking hot chocolate would be nice, but then she stopped and turned, cocking her head.

"What are you all doing home so early anyway? At the same time, even."

One of them being home early was nothing uncommon. But all three at the same time?

There was definitely something up, and the more she caught their gazes and the determination etched in their faces, the more she realized that she was the reason for their early arrival.

Seth caught her hand as she reached for a mug. He gently took the cup away and kissed her forehead. "If you want hot chocolate, I'll get it for you. Why don't you go into the living room? Dillon will build a fire so it's warm. We want to talk to you."

A nervous flutter rose from her belly into her throat. "O-okay."

He gently nudged her in Michael's direction and set about making the hot cocoa. Michael twined his fingers with hers and pulled her toward the living room, where Dillon was already lighting the kindling under the logs in the fireplace.

Michael guided her toward the big, fluffy chair that was her favorite, and she reluctantly let him settle her down. It took all her control not to fidget. She wasn't sure she could sit here calmly and have a rational conversation like they were obviously wanting.

She needed to pace. To work out some of her nervous energy. How could she sit here and look them in the eye when her heart was about to beat out of her chest?

Dillon stood up from his crouch in front of the hearth and turned just as Seth walked in carrying her mug of chocolate. She took it with shaky hands but quickly set it on the table next to her chair before she sloshed it all over herself.

She pushed herself out of the chair, not able to sit still another moment. Michael caught her hand in his firm grasp as if he was afraid to let her go.

"What's wrong, baby?" he asked quietly.

Her first instinct was denial, to say nothing, act as if she had no idea what he was talking about. She tugged her hand away instead and turned, only to land against Dillon's muscled chest.

His agitation was evident in his tense, coiled muscles. For a long moment, he held on to her, his chest heaving against her as he gripped her. He buried his face in her hair and stroked one hand down her back.

"What's going on, Lily?" he asked. "Whatever it is, tell us so we can make you happy again."

She pulled away and smiled. That part was easy even when her insides were in such turmoil. Because all she had to do was think about them and their unwavering love and it brought her instant joy—and peace. Then she reached up to frame his strong jaw. "You always make me happy, Dillon. Always." She took a deep steadying breath before she made her confession. "I'm just scared right now, and I don't know what to do."

He gathered her hands in his and pulled them down between their bodies. His gaze pierced her, right to the heart, so intense. "You don't *ever* have to be afraid."

The vehemence in his voice was reassuring. And she knew. She knew all of this logically. If there was one thing in this world she was sure of was that they'd always protect her and she really didn't have to be afraid. But sometimes logic was so simple. Sometimes fear overran all else. Even common sense.

She swallowed hard and then turned so she could see the others. Seth was staring at her, his blue eyes fierce, but he waited. Tense. Stiff. As if he feared what it was she had to say.

She'd made such a muck of this. Because of her fears, she'd made *them* afraid.

This wasn't the way it should have happened. She should have made a special dinner. Should have asked them how their day went. Snuggled on the couch. Gone to bed, made love, and in the aftermath told them that they were going to be fathers.

And now there was no escape. No do-overs. No way she could pretend nothing was wrong and then plan the big moment for the next night. She'd utterly ruined everything and it was too late to salvage the mess she'd made.

"Talk to us, Lily," Seth pleaded. "We don't like to see you unhappy. Is it . . ." He broke off, rubbed the back of his neck with his palm. Then he dropped his hand and stared back at her with tortured eyes. "Is it us? Are you no longer happy with the arrangement we have?"

Her mouth dropped open in shock. "What? No!" Oh God. It was what they all believed. She'd done this. Made them doubt her commitment because they'd noticed her unhappiness and her distance.

She closed her eyes. "I'm pregnant."

It came out barely a whisper, the words so final. When she opened her eyes, they were staring at her in total surprise.

The multitude of emotions that registered on their faces was hard to track. There was relief. They'd obviously expected something far worse. There was uncertainty, as if they weren't sure they could express their happiness over such news. And there was worry and fear because they knew that of all things, she feared having another child the most.

Seth blew out his breath and wiped a hand over his mouth. He was always, or at least usually, so self-assured. As sheriff he had to be, and he always knew what to say. But now he seemed, for lack of a better word, lost.

Michael looked shell-shocked, and for the first time she realized how just blurting out such news had affected them. Damn it, but she'd just ruined what should have been a special moment. Perhaps one of the most special moments of their lives. She knew how badly they wanted children. A large family like they'd grown up in. They'd been patient and understanding with her fears. They'd never pushed her. Not once. They'd been willing to wait as long as she needed, or to forego having children altogether if that was her wish.

But deep down, she'd known how much they wanted their own family.

Now she'd made a complete and utter mess and she was horrified by her selfishness.

Tears stung her eyes and she put a hand to her mouth to stifle the sob choking her. They'd done so much to make her happy, and she couldn't even give them this one thing without making it sound like the end of the world?

"I'm so sorry," she said in agony. "You didn't deserve this. Not this way."

"Lily," Dillon began.

She shut him out. For the first time she could ever remember, she purposely turned away, closing herself off from her husbands.

She hurried toward the back, wanting—needing— fresh air. To be able to breathe around the huge knot in her throat. So that maybe she wouldn't dissolve into tears or completely break down and lose what little composure she had left.

The cold was a slap in the face, but it was what she needed. Her boots, haphazardly shoved onto her feet, were awkward as she trekked through the snow toward her bench.

She really had no idea where she was going. Or she did, but knew it was no escape. She was so angry at herself for doing this to them.

Of all the ways to tell them that they were going to have a son or daughter, this wasn't one she'd wanted. They would forever associate their firstborn with their mother freaking out and being a selfish twit. Not exactly what she'd want to put into a scrapbook or memory book.

She sank onto the bench and bowed her head, covering her face with her hands.

Almost immediately, warm, strong hands slid over her shoulders. Seth and Michael settled onto the bench next to her while Dillon crouched in front of her. He gently pried her hands away from her face, his expression warm and loving.

"I'm so sorry," she choked out.

"What for? For being human and being scared?" Dillon asked quietly. "Lily, you don't have to put on a brave front with us. You don't have to pretend."

Michael smoothed a hand over her hair and then leaned in to press a kiss to the top of her head. On her other side, Seth slid his hand over hers and laced their fingers together.

"How do you feel about it?" Seth asked softly.

"Scared," she admitted. It felt good to say it out loud. To get it out there. "It caught me off guard. I wasn't prepared and so when I learned that I was for sure pregnant, all the grief over Rose just came back. All the old fears. For a while I was back there in that time, feeling just as I felt then. Exhausted, helpless, alone. Oh God, I don't want to ever feel that way again."

Michael pulled her back into his arms and she laid her head back against his chest while Seth still held tightly to her hand. "I'm sorry, Lily. We were so careful, or we tried to be. You have to know we wouldn't have you feel this way for anything in the world. We just want you to be happy, and if that meant never having a child, we were okay with that."

She appreciated the sentiment, but she was beyond the what-ifs now. She didn't have the luxury of imagining or weighing whether she ever wanted to have another child or not. It was here. Her reality. She was pregnant, and she'd never ever do anything to change that fact.

"I want this baby," she said quietly, fiercely. "I'm scared out of my mind, but I want it. I love him or her already."

A shiver stole over her. Dillon peeled off his coat and arranged it around her body so she would have it and Michael's body for warmth.

Seth raised the hand he still held and kissed her

palm and then each finger. "We'll be here for you, Lily. I need you to trust in that. We'll never let you down. No one will ever be more loved than you and that baby."

Her heart melted and some of the awful fear that had held her captive for so long loosened and slipped away.

"I know. I do trust you. I love you all so very much. I just need some time. To adjust. I'm so sorry I ruined the moment. It should have been special."

Dillon put a finger over her lips. "*You* are what's special to us. It's going to be different this time, Lily. I swear it."

She glanced at the faces of her husbands, at the earnest determination in their eyes. Saw the love— love for her—reflected in their depths.

Yes, it would be different this time, and she had faith—in them, and in herself—that this time her miracle wouldn't slip away.

CHAPTER 9

ADAM Colter watched as his wife, Holly, decorated the huge family Christmas tree with Ethan
and Ryan hovering to make sure she didn't fall off the
ladder.

It's not that they wouldn't have been more than
happy to decorate while she oversaw the project, but
Holly was determined that she hang every ornament
and exclaim over each one as she did so. Every single
one reflected a memory for the Colter family through
the years, and each Christmas the tree grew heavier
with those collected memories.

Maybe it was his age, but he seemed to grow more

nostalgic with each passing year. He'd watched his children grow up under this very roof. He and his brothers had watched their wife blossom under their love and protective umbrella, and in return she'd given them something so infinitely precious that they could never want for more.

Now his children had spread their wings. They'd left the nest and yet they were all right here, surrounding him. All had come back. There had been several points in his life when he couldn't have imagined being happier. The births of his children. Callie being born in the meadow. Holly returning to him and his brothers when they'd thought they'd lost her. But nothing compared to right here, right now.

His wife slipped her arms around his waist and hugged him to her. "What has you so deep in thought over here?"

He blinked, realizing that the tree was done and the lights sparkled like tiny diamonds hung over the thick limbs. He smiled and leaned down to kiss the top of her head.

"I was just thinking about my children and my wife."

Holly turned her face up and smiled back. "Good thoughts then."

"The best."

She sighed and stared back toward the tree and then let her gaze wander to her other husbands as they cleaned up the boxes and put them away until the tree came down.

"This year we'll have Lauren. Callie's so worried about her. She hasn't left Callie and Max's place since she got here a few days ago. Callie says she's so ashamed, and my heart just aches for her. I want to go over and just hug her."

"Why don't you?" Adam asked, smiling at how tenderhearted his beautiful wife was.

Holly hesitated. "Because I know how it feels. That kind of shame. Even as you know it's not yours to bear, you can't shake it."

He squeezed her, anger still fresh and fast to surface when he remembered what she'd endured at her first husband's hands. The little bastard had died in prison the previous year, which only brought a small measure of satisfaction to Adam and his brothers. They would have much preferred to make him suffer a long, slow, painful death.

"It's precisely why you should go visit her," he said softly. "You more than anyone know exactly what she's going through."

"I want her to venture out," Holly said, her lips firming in resolution. "Everyone will spoil her endlessly and restore her faith in the male species. She needs that."

Adam nodded. "Be patient. She'll take on the world and venture out of her safe haven when she's ready. But there's nothing to say that you can't go over and lend her your love and support."

Holly checked her watch and then let out an exclamation. "I've got to run. I'm supposed to go see Lily today."

"I'll drive you," Ethan said from across the room. "I need to go into town anyway."

Holly frowned and shook her head. "No need."

Adam exchanged raised eyebrows with his brothers. Holly had been acting awfully suspicious lately. Not that she didn't often visit Lily, but during the last week, she'd gone down there with increasing frequency and she was adamant that no one accompany her.

Ryan's lips thinned and he crossed his arms over his chest as though he was about to argue, but then he seemed to think better of it and abruptly backed down. "What time will you be back?" he asked gruffly. "It's supposed to snow again."

Holly considered the matter a moment and then

did another check of her watch. "I'll be home by dark. Promise. I may stop in to check on Callie—and Lauren, but I'll call you from her house if I do."

Adam pulled her up and kissed her lingeringly. "Be careful, okay? We worry when you're away from us."

She shot him a dazzling smile and hurried away to get her purse and keys. As soon as she left the room, Adam shot his brothers a seeking glance.

"What the hell is our sweet little wife up to?"

Ethan shook his head. "Hell if I know, but she scares me when she gets this way. There's no telling what she has up her sleeve."

Ryan frowned and shoved his hands into his pockets. "You think everything is okay with Lily? Have the boys said anything lately about any problems they might be having? Holly's been spending a lot of time with her lately."

Adam rubbed his hand over his chin as he pondered the possibility. But no. Seth, Michael, and Dillon all seemed happy. Content. At total peace. You could sense it in them. And there'd been nothing in Lily's actions to hint at any turmoil. She was as sweet as ever. Quiet, shy, but fierce in her protection of the people she loved.

Finally he shrugged. "It does us no good to stand

around and speculate. Sooner or later we'll know what she's up to. Until then we'll just have to be patient."

HOLLY pulled into Callie's driveway just as dusk was blanketing the mountains. Snow flurries spun and spiraled in crazy swirls, melting on the windshield as she cut the engine. Instead of calling her husbands as she'd promised, she sent a text to all three that she was safe at Callie's and would be home shortly. It saved time and prevented the inevitable concern she'd hear in their voices.

And to be honest, she wasn't feeling entirely wonderful. She had a chill and a fiery ache had settled into her right side. The fever could well be the result of being exposed to Callie's strep throat, and she could only assume she'd eaten something over the past several days that hadn't agreed with her. She and Lily had cooked enough Christmas dinners to feed an entire battalion. Twice. But she was confident that come Christmas Day, she was going to serve her family the best holiday dinner they'd ever tasted.

With a sigh, she climbed out of the SUV and headed toward Callie's front door. The entire front of Callie's house was decorated in bright, colorful Christmas lights. A large wreath hung on the door, and framed in the huge picture window stood the tree, ablaze with over a thousand white lights. Callie had always loved Christmas. Every bit as much as Holly did. It warmed Holly through that her daughter had her own home just a short distance away from her parents. She missed her babies when they were away and of all her children, Callie had spent the most time away from home. Now she was back where she belonged and Max would keep her centered. He'd calmed her restless spirit and had given her a safe haven.

As she reached the steps, the porch light came on and the door opened, revealing Max.

"Hello, Mrs. C. Come in, come in. Here, let me take your coat."

"Hi Max," Holly said, leaning up on tiptoe to kiss his cheek. Her son-in-law's acceptance into the family hadn't come without hiccups, but he'd proven himself a dozen times over since he and Callie had married.

Max took her coat and ushered her inside to the living room, where a fire blazed in the hearth.

"Mom!" Callie cried as she hurried over.

Holly caught her daughter in her arms and hugged her tightly. "Hi, baby. How are you?"

"I'm good. What brings you over? Would you like some hot chocolate or a glass of wine?"

"Nothing for me, thank you," Holly said. "Where's Lauren? I'd hoped to see her while I was here."

Callie and Max exchanged pained looks.

"She's in her room," Callie said with a sigh.

Holly glanced at Max. "Would you mind if I went to see her?"

Max wiped a hand wearily over his face. "I'd be grateful for whatever you could do for her. I feel so damn helpless. I want to help her but I don't know how. She's hurting and I'm powerless to stop it."

Holly impulsively went to him and enfolded him a big hug. In her mind, no one ever got too old for a motherly hug, and judging by his reaction, he didn't think so either.

He hugged her back, squeezing a little tighter than normal.

Holly drew away and patted his cheek affectionately. "I know you don't feel like you're helping her, Max, but I promise you she appreciates you just being here and for going to New York to fight for her. She's adrift. She feels isolated and alone. She's afraid, ashamed, angry. It just takes time to heal and to regain your confidence."

"If she can be as half as strong as you are, Mrs. C, she'll be just fine," Max said, clear love in his voice.

"I wasn't very strong in the beginning," Holly said ruefully. "Adam, Ethan, and Ryan made me strong. Their *love* made me strong. Just like our love is going to make Lauren strong again. We simply have to make her see it."

"Thank you," Max said sincerely. "For caring about my sister."

Holly smiled, reached over to squeeze Callie's hand, and then headed toward the stairs. "I'll be back down in a bit, Callie. If your fathers call, tell them I'm with Lauren. They'll understand."

She climbed the stairs and turned to the left, away from the master suite and down a hallway where the other bedrooms were located. At the end, she encountered the closed door of Lauren's bedroom and knocked softly.

"Lauren? It's Holly Colter. Can I come in for a few minutes?"

A long moment later, the door opened and Lauren stood there, surprise and confusion reflected in her dark, wounded eyes. Holly wanted to cry as she took in how changed the lovely young woman was from the last time Holly had visited with her.

She looked infinitely fragile. Haunted. Callie had said she'd been wearing scarves and long sleeves to cover the bruises, but she wore no such things now, and even days after her attack, there was still evidence of bruising. Much fainter now. Yellow and green instead of black and blue, but the marks were there.

"Hi," Holly offered softly.

Lauren smiled but swallowed nervously. "Hi, Mrs. Colter. I didn't realize you were coming over."

Holly flashed a bright, cheerful smile, determined not to show any pity or anger over Lauren's condition. "Oh, I pop in all the time. I wanted to see how you were doing. I've been dying to see you again."

Guilt crept into Lauren's eyes and she gripped the door a little tighter.

"Can I come in?" Holly asked again.

Lauren hastily glanced back and then opened the door wide. "Of course. I'm sorry."

Holly sailed past her, her heart aching at the change so evident in the young woman. Spying the two chairs by the window, she headed in that direction and perched on the edge of one. She leaned over to pat the other and motioned for Lauren to sit.

Lauren gingerly settled onto the opposite chair, her

unease rippling from her in waves. Holly grasped Lauren's hands and squeezed comfortingly.

"I've never been good at being subtle so I'm going to just dive right in. Callie told me what happened to you."

Lauren closed her eyes and her head bowed automatically. Holly moved one of her hands from Lauren's and cupped Lauren's chin, gently nudging it upward until Lauren was forced to look at her.

"Listen to me, baby," Holly said in an achingly gentle voice. "This wasn't your fault. It's not your shame to bear. I know how you're feeling. I understand all too well."

Lauren's eyes clouded. "How?" she cracked out. "How could you possibly know? Or understand? Your husbands would never . . ."

Holly shook her head. "No, they wouldn't. Thank God for that. I thank God for them every single day. But you know what? I didn't always have them. I was running from my first husband when Adam found me lying in a ditch. He took me home, and he and his brothers helped put me back together. They protected me, they loved me, and they gave me the strength to fight back when the time came."

Lauren's eyes rounded in surprise. "You . . . Someone—your husband—hurt you?"

Holly nodded. "Lauren, honey, you can't hide from the world forever, and moreover, you can't hide from the people who love you. My husbands and my sons are dying to spoil you rotten and treat you like an honorary daughter and sister. Hell, they spoil Callie shamelessly and she's a married, grown woman. It's bad enough Max gives her the moon, but her fathers and brothers do as well. I know it's hard for you to trust right now, but in time your faith will be restored. Not all men are bastards. There are some really good men out there who'd die before ever hurting a woman."

Tears filled Lauren's eyes. "I just feel so stupid. And I'm angry with myself. I should have left him. I made excuses for him. I brushed off the warning signs. I just felt so damn alone and for a while he filled that emptiness inside me."

"Oh, honey," Holly said, pulling Lauren into her arms. She held her tightly and rocked back and forth. "It isn't a crime to make a mistake. We all make them. Just because you gave your trust to the wrong man doesn't mean you should punish yourself for the rest of your life."

Lauren sighed and wiped hastily at her tears as she pulled away from Holly. "It sounds pretty stupid when you say it like that. What I mean is that I sound stupid and you make complete sense. I just wish it was that easy to believe, you know?"

Holly smiled and ran her hand over Lauren's damp cheek. "The thing is, you don't have to endure this alone. You're surrounded by family, by people who love you. No one in this family thinks less of you. We're worried about you. My boys want to go kick the little bastard's ass, but we all just want you to be happy again. Venture out of your shell. We want you to feel safe here."

This time Lauren hugged Holly and her slender body shook with sobs as she buried her face in Holly's shoulder. For the longest time, Holly simply sat there and held her, rocking her back and forth as Lauren let go of the pent-up emotion.

"I miss my mom," Lauren whispered.

"I know you do, baby. It's times like these when a girl needs her mother the most. No matter how old you get, the need for your mother never goes away. I hope you'll allow me to stand in for her."

Lauren squeezed her fiercely. "I'd love that more than anything."

Holly squeezed her back. "Not only do you have a stand-in mother, but you also have three fathers and three brothers in addition to Max, and you have two sisters too."

Lauren lifted her head, her eyes wide in wonder. "I do, don't I?"

Holly smiled. "You most certainly do."

"Oh," Lauren breathed. "Max and I are so very lucky. For so long it was just us three. Him, me, and Mama. And then just me and Max. I've always dreamed of having a big, loving, wonderful family that just surrounded me."

"Well, I'd say you got your wish," Holly said with an indulgent smile.

Lauren wiped at her face again and briefly looked down before returning her gaze to Holly. "Does the self-recrimination ever go away? I close my eyes at night and I'm just bombarded by humiliation. I cringe at the things I put up with. Don't get me wrong, I'm furious with him. But I'm also angry with myself, and that's harder to take."

"You're being too hard on yourself," Holly said gently. "Give yourself time to heal. Distance always provides perspective. The guilt and self-blame will fade. You'll be able to look back and know that the blame lies solely with him."

"I hope you're right," Lauren murmured. "I hate wallowing in this cesspool of pity."

"My advice? Get out more. Stop shutting yourself away from the world. Take long walks. It's beautiful up here. Go to town. Buy something fun for yourself. Pamper yourself. Get a manicure. Whatever it takes to give yourself back the gift of confidence."

Lauren smiled. "Thanks, Mrs. C. Really, just thank you. I needed this kick in the ass."

"Oh, I don't kick people in the ass," Holly said. "That's what my husbands are for. I just hug people to death and then mother them senseless."

Impulsively, Lauren hugged her again. "I'm so glad I'm here. This family is the absolute best."

Holly held her for a long moment and then eased back so she could rise from her chair. "I'd love for you to come up to the house for dinner. My children are in and out all the time. Our door is always open."

"I'd like that," Lauren said softly.

"And now I better run before the husbands send out a search party," she said in amusement.

"They love you so much," Lauren said wistfully.

Holly reached out to stroke her hair. "One day you'll find someone who loves you just as much."

"I'll walk you down," Lauren said, rising from her own chair.

Holly gave her a delighted smile. Max and Callie would be thrilled that Lauren ventured down. It was a step. Lauren wouldn't be taking on the world in the next day, but she'd get there on her own. The Colters would simply close ranks around her and help her get back on her feet again.

CHAPTER 10

LILY waited anxiously for her husbands to get home. They'd been banished to the dads so Holly could come over for her cooking lesson. For the first time, Lily had been impatient for her mother-in-law to leave. Lily was focused on having her men return so that she could make things right.

She thought back over her plan for the hundredth time, reciting the words she'd committed to memory but also knowing that the moment her husbands were there in front of her, she'd forget everything and have to wing it.

The important thing was that she would give them

a memory to replace the one of her freaking out and scaring them to death. She'd give them something to look back on when their own children were grown. A happy time, a time to be excited and look to the future.

It had been a wake-up call for her when she'd realized just how much she lived in the now. Not that it was a bad thing. No one wanted to wish their life away, always looking forward and never enjoying the here and now.

But she'd made it a practice to never look beyond the next day. It was almost as if she were afraid to hope for any kind of a future. Or maybe she was just afraid she wouldn't have one.

Finding out she was pregnant had altered her perception. It had altered her focus. No longer was today the only thing she concentrated on. Now she looked to the future, imagining how their lives would change when they welcomed a son or daughter into their family.

It was . . . nice.

Scary. Heart-stopping. Nerve-racking. But so very nice.

Her pulse leaped when she heard the truck in the drive. She smoothed her hands down her jeans, wiping her palms before she started toward the door to greet them.

She was there to open the door before they reached the porch. She tried to smile but she was so nervous that she wasn't sure she pulled it off convincingly.

Michael reached her first, and before he could say anything, she launched herself into his arms and gave him a scorching kiss to curl his toes.

When she pulled away, his eyes were half-lidded and dazed. She smiled and pushed him into the living room.

Seth and Dillon stood in the doorway, observing her cautiously. Not wanting to leave them out in the least, she went into Seth's arms and kissed him with every bit as much heat as she'd kissed Michael.

Man, she loved the way he smelled. Loved the way he felt. He was still wearing his uniform, and he hadn't yet taken off his holster with his gun.

All in good time.

She felt a little smug when he was reluctant to let her go, but she pointed him toward Michael and then went into Dillon's arms.

She tried to take control much as she'd done with Michael and Seth—though interestingly enough, Michael was the more dominant force, especially when it came to sex—but Dillon was having none of that.

He met her hungrily, taking over and ravaging her mouth. For several long, breathless seconds, he tasted her, explored her lips, and nibbled teasingly at their fullness.

"How are you feeling?" he whispered.

She put a finger over his lips and then turned to the others.

"I have something important I want to tell you."

Seth lifted an eyebrow, then glanced at Michael, then to Dillon, and finally back to her. "Okay."

She gestured everyone toward the couch. "Sit."

As soon as they were all seated, she moved forward, no longer nervous or edgy. Peace settled over her. Her mind was quiet and no longer contained the painful memories of the past. It was filled instead with images of the future. Of her husbands and a tiny newborn baby. And then an older child, a girl or a boy. And of her husbands doting on him or her, and other children. Their family.

Her heart felt near to bursting. For so long she'd been ruled by the past. She'd hurt for so long that she'd nearly forgotten how to experience joy. Now it flooded her. Seeped into every part of her heart and soul.

She went to her knees between Dillon's legs and reached with both hands to pull Seth's and Michael's hands so that she held them against her heart.

"Guess what? I'm having your baby," she said, her smile so big that she could barely get the words out.

Seth's eyes went soft. With love. So much love. And understanding as well. Michael smiled and squeezed her hand. Dillon reached out and cupped her cheek, his expression so fierce, and yet tears glittered harshly in his eyes.

"Isn't that wonderful?" she asked.

And suddenly she was pulled onto Dillon's lap. Michael cradled her from behind and Seth pulled her feet onto his lap. They surrounded her, their love warming her to her very core.

"It's the most wonderful gift anyone's ever given me," Dillon choked out.

Seth's hand caressed a line up her leg to rest on her knee and he squeezed, his smile so big that his face nearly split.

Michael nuzzled her neck and then whispered low in her ear. "Are you happy, Lily? I know you're scared, baby, but are you happy?"

She turned, leaning into his chest. "I'm terrified, but I've never been happier than at this moment."

"We won't let you down," Dillon said gruffly. "We'll be with you every second of every minute of every day. You'll never be alone."

She reached up to cup his face as he'd done to hers. "I know, Dillon. I do know. I love you all so much. I'm so sorry I handled this so badly the first time. I wanted it to be special and for a little while, I let grief for Rose overwhelm me. I want this baby. I want our child. So very much."

She turned so she could straddle Dillon's lap and so she could touch Michael and Seth. She could see them and they could see her.

"Before I met you, I would never have believed that my life could be so full of joy and happiness. I'd vowed to never have another child. I wouldn't risk it. But you give me such strength. You love me, and because you love me, I feel so strong. I feel like I can do *anything*. Even face my darkest fear."

Seth leaned in and pressed his lips to hers and then he cupped the back of her head, simply holding her close.

"We'll do this together, Lily. Just like Dillon said. You'll never be alone. We'll be with you every step of the way. Our baby will be protected, cherished, and loved by every member of the Colter family. No child will ever grow up more loved."

"Have you been to the doctor yet?" Michael asked. "Do you know how far along you are?"

They hadn't discussed the pregnancy since she'd had her little meltdown. She could see the questions they were dying to ask, but they'd purposely not overwhelmed her and had given her time to adjust to the idea.

She loved them for that, but she also knew that it had been difficult for them because they wanted to be able to talk about it. They wanted to be able to be excited. They wanted her to be as happy about it as they were.

And so they'd let her take the lead and had been as loving and supportive as always, content to wait until she was ready to take that first shaky step.

Well, she was there. She might not light the world on fire with her courage or bravery, but she had something going for her that not many others had. She had three wonderful men who loved her unconditionally.

Unconditionally.

Such a strong, powerful word. How many people could say they were loved without conditions? Without strings? No questions. No hesitation. They were *loved*.

Her heart clutched even as she nodded in response to Michael's question.

"I went to see Dr. Burton several days ago. I suspected . . . or rather I had a suspicion, or maybe it was a fear. He did a test there in the office, then gave me a bunch of vitamins to take and scheduled another appointment in a month. My best estimate is that I'm around six to eight weeks along. Probably closer to eight by now."

"We'll all go with you to your appointments. Every one of them. Have you been feeling sick? Are you more tired than usual?"

Lily smiled at the concern in Michael's voice. Though as a vet he treated animals, he still went all doctorly on her at the first sign of any illness or upset.

"Queasy. And yes, tired. Like oh-my-God tired. And my breasts are sore. But the fatigue was what clued me in. It was exactly how I felt with Rose—like I didn't even want to get out of bed. I felt that way for much of my pregnancy, and it's why I never really recovered when I went home with her."

Dillon's expression grew fierce. "That won't happen this time. You're going to rest. You aren't going to lift a finger. And after the baby is born, you're coming home and you're not going to do anything more than hold or feed the baby."

Her heart ached at the protectiveness in his voice. If only she'd had them when Rose was born. So many if-onlys. She reached down to place a hand on her still-flat belly. She couldn't bring Rose back. And she couldn't replace her. But she could give birth to her brother or sister, and a part of Rose would live on.

Dillon picked up her hand and pressed a gentle kiss to her palm. "I love you, Lily. We'll take care of you and our baby. I swear it."

She leaned forward and hugged him tightly. He wrapped his arms around her and held on. He trembled against her, so much emotion shuddering through his big body.

"I know you will, Dillon. I love you too. So much. You and Michael and Seth saved me. You save me every day."

When she pulled away, Michael tugged her into his arms and cradled her close.

"Do you want to tell the rest of the family or would you rather wait awhile?"

Lily hesitated. "I thought it would be a great Christmas present. For everyone. A new Colter. The first grandchild for your parents. Everyone will be together this year. Somehow it just seems fitting to break the news then."

"I think that's a wonderful idea," Seth said, joy lighting his eyes.

"You know what I think would be an even more wonderful idea?" she said in a low, husky voice.

Dillon's hands tightened on her thighs as though he recognized the tone in her voice and knew exactly what it was she was up to.

"What's that?" Dillon asked in a near growl.

"If you all took me to bed and made love to me."

"Oh hell yes," Michael said as he rose from the couch. He was already reaching for her, pulling her up from Dillon's lap.

He swept her into his arms, cradling her against his heart. He gazed down at her, relief and love like a beacon shining in his eyes.

"I love you," he said, his voice hoarse and a little shaky.

She reached up to touch his face. "I love you too."

He carried her toward the bedroom, followed by Seth and Dillon. Once there, he laid her gently on the bed and kissed her deep and sweet.

There was a reverence to their every touch as they

undressed her. Their touches were gentle, so much so that it made her chest tighten and ache. Their fingers stroked, their palms caressed, and their lips kissed.

She lay there naked, spread out before them as they stood over the bed, their gazes riveted. Their eyes brimmed with love, with adoration. Tears burned her lids because she could feel their love. They didn't just say the words. They lived them each and every day.

It had nearly broken her when Seth had asked if she no longer wanted the relationship with him and his brothers. *Never* did she want them to doubt her love or her commitment.

She watched as they undressed. She never tired of seeing their bodies, of holding her breath as each piece of clothing fell away. They still did that to her. Still made her light-headed and turned her on with nothing more than a stare.

Michael was the leanest of the three. Taut, muscled. Not as broad shouldered as his brothers, but he was a bit taller. While Seth and Dillon had short, clean haircuts, Michael had shoulder-length, mussed hair that she found adorably sexy. She always thought it was his one rebellion. Nothing about him would make anyone think he was a rebel. He was extremely intelligent, quiet, and tended to be serious.

Seth was broader and his muscles more developed. He maintained a disciplined fitness regimen, especially since he'd been laid up and out of work for several months after being shot two years ago.

Dillon was the stockiest of the three. Massive shoulders, bulging arms that sported tattoos. He had an I-don't-give-a-fuck attitude that often irritated others, but those who knew him knew he had a heart of gold and when he loved, he loved with all his heart, deeply and without reservation. He was loyal to his toes. All the Colters were. It was a principle drilled into them from birth.

Family wasn't just something. It was *everything*.

Dillon leaned over her, pressing his hard, warm body to hers. He was careful to hold most of his weight off her as he stared down into her eyes. He stroked his fingers through her hair and then leaned down to kiss her.

"Are you more sensitive now?" he asked huskily. "I've heard women's breasts can be painful during early pregnancy."

She smiled. "Yeah, they're extremely tender. They feel bigger, and if I so much as bump into something, it's like stubbing a toe."

"Then we'll be extra careful with you."

He moved to the side of her, laid back, and then reached for her arm. "Get on top," he coaxed. "I want to look at you, and I know they do too."

Seth took her hand and helped her sit up, and then Michael was there, helping her slide over Dillon's thighs. She settled just below his straining erection, allowing it to rest against her belly.

No one could resist such temptation.

She wrapped her fingers around the thick base and gently slid her hand upward to the tip. The bed dipped and Michael and Seth got in on either side of her. Seth leaned in, kissing her shoulder, nipping gently. Michael cupped one breast ever so gently in his palm, then leaned down to brush a light kiss across the top.

Her nipple immediately hardened and instead of aching discomfort, she ached for his touch. She wanted his mouth, even knowing how hypersensitive her breasts were at the moment.

Dillon slid his hands up her legs and over her hips to her waist. Then he lifted her, positioning her so she was over his cock.

There was a sense of urgency, almost as if he couldn't wait to get inside her, to reaffirm his possession. As soon as she pushed down, enveloping his hardness, his nostrils flared and his eyes closed.

His hands shook at her hips and then he tightened his grip as she took him all.

Seth turned her face to his, kissing her long and deep. "Is it okay? He's not hurting you, is he?"

She returned his kiss hungrily, wanting more. She wanted it all. All three men loving and cherishing her. Making love to her as only they could.

"No," she whispered. "But I want more. I want you."

Seth sucked in his breath. "Are you sure?"

She nodded. "You won't hurt me, Seth. The baby is safe. We don't have to stop making love. At least not for a while. I need you."

The soft plea turned his eyes warm and soft but then they glittered and his pupils dilated. His breathing sped up as he pulled back and pushed up from the bed. A moment later he returned and rained a trail of kisses down her spine, to the small of her back, and then over the curve of her behind.

His fingers were gentle as he parted her cheeks. The lubricant was warm, as if he'd rubbed it between his hands so it wouldn't be cold. His fingers slid easily inward, easing the passageway.

For several breathless moments, she remained still, mounted on top of Dillon, whose cock was hard and deep within her. She tried not to move as Seth's fingers worked sensuously in and out of her tight opening.

Her pussy tightened around Dillon's cock with each stroke of Seth's hand and Dillon groaned, his fingers digging into her waist.

Michael stayed to her other side as Seth carefully positioned himself at her entrance. Michael stroked her hair, caressed her breast with featherlike touches, and then bent down to run his tongue over the taut peak.

She sighed, or maybe it was a moan. She was edgy and itchy all over. Eager, impatient. They were being so incredibly careful and she loved them for it. Maybe she even needed this gentleness from them when she felt so vulnerable.

They weren't in any hurry, and they seemed determined that each movement fully express how much they adored her.

"I want to taste you," she whispered against Michael's lips as he returned to kiss her.

He smiled but shook his head. "This is all for you, baby. We're not taking. We're giving. I'm just going to stay right here and I'm going to kiss you and tell you how much I love you while Seth and Dillon bring you as much pleasure as they can. And then afterward, I'm going to hold you and our child while you sleep."

The beauty and sincerity of his words clutched at her heart. She reached over, thrust her hand into his hair, and pulled him closer so she could lock her lips to his as Seth slid past the resistance of her body.

She gasped into Michael's mouth. The sudden fullness was overwhelming, as it always was. No matter how often they took her in this fashion, the thrill never wore off. It was always as exciting as the very first time.

"Tell me how it feels," Michael growled into her mouth. "Tell me what it feels like to have them both inside you."

"Like heaven," she whispered. "I so love when all three of you are a part of me. Inside me. Showing me your love and allowing me to show you mine."

Michael's hand fisted in her hair just as Seth and Dillon found their rhythm. Dillon held her more gently now, his hands on her hips, holding her in place for their combined thrusts.

Her eyes were half-lidded as she stared into Michael's eyes. Her hair was drawn tight, the strands wrapped around his fingers as he held his fist firm.

"Please," she begged softly.

Michael blew out his breath in a ragged spurt. "Like I could damn well refuse you anything."

He maneuvered up, standing and leaning back toward the headboard. Then, using one hand as leverage against the wall and leaving the other tightly wound in her hair, he pushed his hips forward until his cock pressed against her mouth.

She ran her tongue over the tip, appreciating the moan that spilled from his lips. Then she sucked him inside, wanting that last connection.

They were all three a part of her. Deep inside her.

She relaxed, allowing the tension to ease and the fear that had knotted her insides for so long to slide away.

She let them take the reins. Let them have control. She trusted them. She was in their hands. In their care.

Closing her eyes, she inhaled deeply and took Michael as far as she could, savoring the taste and feel of him on her tongue.

Seth slid deeper into her body in an alternating rhythm with Dillon. When Seth pulled back, Dillon sank deep. When Dillon retreated, Seth pushed forward.

Their movements were exquisitely tender. No hurry. No frantic race to completion. It was as if they'd determined that they had all the time in the world and they weren't rushing a damn thing.

Dillon's hands left her hips and trailed up her belly, pausing for a moment to caress her abdomen. Then he went higher, palming both of her breasts in the most tender of gestures.

He ran both thumbs lightly over the puckered nipples, all the while making sure he didn't press too hard.

"Touch yourself, Lily," he said huskily.

Having long since lost her self-consciousness when it came to lovemaking, she lowered one hand to Dillon's taut abdomen and then trailed her fingers down to his groin where their bodies met and meshed.

She slid her fingers between them, through damp folds, until she stroked over her clitoris.

Immediately her body tightened all over. Seth and Dillon both let out strangled sounds. Her mouth molded tighter around Michael's cock and his fingers tangled in her hair once more, holding her in place while he stroked back and forth over her tongue.

"That's it," Dillon murmured. "Pleasure yourself. I want to see you come apart right in front of my eyes. I want to feel you tighten all around my dick and then bathe me in your heat."

Her nostrils flared and her body began to tremble

all over in response to the seductive words. Dillon had such a wicked tongue. He had a way with words that never failed to tilt her right over the edge. He could talk a woman to orgasm. She was convinced of it.

Seth's hands gripped her behind, held her as he began to thrust more forcefully.

She was teetering. So close. So very close.

She rubbed her clit in a circular motion, stroking the taut, sensitive bud with one finger. Harder. Faster.

The world went hazy around her. All she was aware of was pleasure. Beautiful, never-ending pleasure. And the love of the three men who'd changed her life forever.

Inside her. All of them. Deep. Loving.

She let out a soft cry around Michael's erection and then went liquid in their arms. Seth and Dillon both held her up, supporting her with gentle hands.

Michael slid out of her mouth, though she knew he hadn't come, and she slumped forward onto Dillon's chest as Seth shuddered behind her, in the throes of his own orgasm.

Dillon twitched, arched his hips up one last time and then he closed his eyes and wrapped his arms solidly around her, holding her as he poured himself into her body.

For the longest time, she lay there, softly panting, eyes closed as she savored the aftermath. All too soon, Dillon shifted and then she found herself lifted into Michael's arms. He turned, rolling with her so she was nestled into his side on the bed.

She snuggled into his embrace, tangling her legs with his. She wanted to be close. Didn't want any space between them.

And then Seth was behind her, molding himself to her back, one leg thrown over hers so she was completely and utterly surrounded by him and Michael.

She smiled against Michael's neck. This was love. This was her life.

This was home.

CHAPTER 11

CALLIE sat at the vanity in her bedroom brushing her hair, but her gaze never left Max as he shrugged out of his shirt and prepared to go shower.

He wouldn't take long. He never did. Not when he showered alone. Which he'd been doing with increasing frequency lately.

Usually . . . She stroked through her hair again and frowned as she watched him disappear into the bathroom. Usually he took her into the shower, washed her hair and every inch of her body. Then and only then did he quickly see to his own shower, and when they were done, he'd dry her body and her hair and then she'd await his next instruction.

Chill bumps danced across her skin at the memory of some of those instructions.

One simply never knew with Max.

His power and his confidence enticed her. His dominance gave her a measure of comfort nothing else could.

In his arms, she was free to be herself. He was her center, her anchor. A safe haven for her free spirit and wanderlust. Because no matter where she went, where she was, if she was with Max, she was home.

She continued to brush her hair even though there wasn't a single knot and the strands were starting to fuzz out from static electricity. She was waiting. For Max.

Max wasn't himself, but then she could hardly blame him. His focus was on Lauren. But what Callie didn't like was the way Max seemed to be pushing Callie away.

She understood his worry and his concern. Knew that he was preoccupied with thoughts of his sister. But Callie was his wife and they were supposed to share everything. She knew without a doubt that if she had a family issue, he'd be by her side, involved up to his nose, and he'd do whatever he had to in order to help or support her.

She looked up when the door to the bathroom opened. Max stepped out still toweling his hair dry and wearing only a towel around his waist.

Her mouth went dry because the man was simply gorgeous. He still took her breath away. Still made her heart do this silly little stutter step every time she looked his way.

She laid the brush down and then turned on her seat to face him. He tossed aside the towel he'd been using to dry his hair and then seemed to realize she was looking at him.

He caught her gaze and then his brow furrowed. "Is something wrong?"

She didn't answer right away. Nervous butterflies scuttled around her belly before her chin finally came up and she felt calm descend.

"Why are you avoiding me, Max?"

His eyes widened in surprise that wasn't faked. "Avoid you? Where the hell would you get an idea like that?"

She rose and walked toward him. She allowed her

robe to fall away until she stood naked before him. Then she gracefully slid to her knees, lifting her chin so she could once more look him in the eye.

"You're avoiding this," she said softly. "Us. The way we are. *Who* we are. Have you changed your mind, Max? Is this no longer what you want?"

She pulled at one of the bands around her wrist, the implication being that she'd remove it even though she couldn't without one of the tiny keys they both owned, but his hand was quick to clamp around her wrist, holding the band tightly in place.

"No!" he said hoarsely. "God no, Callie, don't take it off. Those mean more than our wedding rings. Is this what you want? Is this what you're trying to tell me?"

She stayed on her knees, his fingers still wrapped tightly around her wrist.

"You haven't touched me," she said quietly. "I understand why you wouldn't demonstrate your dominance of me in front of Lauren or others. We agreed that what we do is private and not for the world to see. But even in the privacy of our bedroom, you've stopped . . . you've stopped everything. What am I to think other than that this isn't what *you* want?"

He went to his knees in front of her, only the second

time ever that he'd put himself in an equally vulnerable position with her. He grasped her face between his hands, his eyes dark and earnest.

"You are my *life*, Callie. If anything I've said or done has made you doubt that even for a moment, I'm sorry. I would never have you feel that way."

She shook her head because this wasn't about her pouting and being dramatic. She didn't want to bring him low. She just wanted her Max back. Dominant, badass Max who always had a firm hand with her.

"I just want to know what's changed. Is it Lauren? Do I need to spell it out? We're currently existing just like a normal couple with an average marriage and an average sex life. We aren't normal, Max. I submit to you. I choose to submit. Wholly. With no reservations. That doesn't mean sometimes or when I feel like it. It's always. I made that commitment. It's what I need. It's what I want. But ever since we brought Lauren home, you've done everything but act the dominant counterpart. If anything, you've backed way off and have been careful not to seem remotely demanding in any aspect of our relationship."

Max leaned his forehead against Callie's and she felt the tremor of emotion flow through his body and into hers.

Slowly he rose and then extended his hand down to her. Wordlessly. Just a look that told her it wasn't a request. Relief surged, making her shaky as she allowed him to pull her to her feet. He led her to the bed, pulled the covers back, and then motioned for her to crawl in.

He then sat on the edge, his body angled so he faced her. His expression was serious and a little uncertain. This wasn't the Max she was used to.

"When I saw her," he said in a low voice. "When I saw the bruises, when she told me what happened and she explained the relationship she had with this asshole, it sickened me. And then I began to think, is this me? Am I like that?"

Callie gasped. Of all the things she thought might be wrong, this certainly hadn't been a consideration. It horrified her that Max was mentally comparing himself to the man who'd abused his sister.

He shook his head, a silent command for her to remain quiet.

"I'm controlling. You know this. I know this. From the day we met, I took over. I took, you gave. I dominated, you submitted. Some of the things that we do . . . God, Callie, can you imagine how someone looking in from the outside would view our relationship? Can you imagine if Lauren walked in when you're across my lap and I'm spanking your ass? Or when I have you tied up and I'm fucking your ass after I've reddened it with a crop? How do you think that would look to her? Hell, she'd be calling nine-one-one."

Callie swallowed hard but remained silent as he continued.

"Do you know what would happen if one of your fathers or your brothers ever saw the marks on your body from one of our encounters? You have to know that I'm extremely careful with placement so that you don't have to answer uncomfortable questions to your family and so they won't come after me with a shotgun. Because if they ever so much as thought that I was hurting you, they'd kill me, *dolcezza*. They'd do it without remorse."

"Oh Max," she whispered. "Don't you see the difference?"

Max closed his eyes. "I used to see it. Or rather, I thought I did. I told myself that I loved you and that you loved me and that this was a consensual relationship. I justified it in my head. I made excuses. But then

I really looked hard and I asked myself what made me any different than the bastard who put those bruises on Lauren's body?"

Callie leaned forward, cupping Max's jaw in her palm. With her other hand, she laced her fingers through his and brought his hand up until it lay against her heart.

"When you aren't so raw with grief over what's happened to Lauren, you'll realize how very different the situations are. You do nothing that I don't want. You do nothing that we haven't agreed upon. I can say no at any time. You pamper and spoil me endlessly. You take care of me. You give me everything I could ever possibly need or want. And you love me.

"He didn't love Lauren. He wanted to control her. He wanted to hurt her. He wanted to intimidate her. To him she was a thing. Something to vent his temper on. When have you ever touched me in anger? When have you ever lost control and struck me in anger?"

Max still looked indecisive and tortured.

"Are you trying to say that I don't know the difference between love and abuse?" she asked softly. "That I don't have a mind of my own and that you do all my thinking for me? That I'm just a puppet dancing on your strings? That I obey without question or that I'm too afraid to stand up to you?"

He visibly recoiled. "Hell no. You're one of the strongest willed women I know."

She smiled then and caressed the lines on his face. "Then tell me how on earth you think you'd ever get away with abusing me. Forget my dads and my brothers. If you ever crossed the line, it isn't them you'd need to worry about. It's me, because I'd kick your fucking ass all over this mountain. There wouldn't be anything left for my fathers or brothers to mangle when I was finished with you."

His expression eased and his lips twitched upward into a smile.

"So what you're telling me is that I'm being a complete idiot."

"Well, yes, I suppose that's exactly what I'm saying," she said with a grin.

He gathered her in his arms and held her tightly, his face buried in her hair. "I love you, Callie. So damn much. I don't want to ever be without you. I couldn't live with myself if I ever hurt you, if I ever abused your trust in me."

She nestled her face in his neck, inhaling his scent.

When he finally pulled away, his face was somber. "I don't know what to do to help her, Callie. For the first several days I felt like the worst sort of fraud. God, I felt ashamed, like I was some hypocrite and that I wasn't worthy of any better treatment than the son of a bitch who beat her."

Callie smiled softly, allowing her love to shine through. "Just being here for her is helping. Us going to get her, not allowing her to close herself off and wallow in shame—that's helping. She's going to be fine. It'll take time. The best thing you can do is not treat her like she's broken. Don't tiptoe around her. Treat her like she's part of the family and that we're thrilled she's here. The rest will come in time."

Max let his hand wander through her hair and then down to her bare breasts, where he toyed idly with her nipples. "Has anyone ever told you that you're a wise woman, Callie Wilder?"

She laughed. "No, I can honestly say that no one in my family has ever accused me of being anything but flighty and free-spirited. Wise doesn't exactly fit in there anywhere."

He kissed her temple and squeezed her tight again. "You're my everything, *dolcezza*. And where you fit is right here with me. Always."

"Then don't hold back," she begged. "I need you, Max. I need your dominance, your strength. Your control. I need that structure. It centers me. It reminds me that I have a place in this world. With you."

He let his hands slide down to the bands circling her wrists. The bands he'd placed there as a symbol of his ownership. To him, they were more important than their wedding rings. They meant more. They went deeper.

"Never take these off," he said quietly. "I couldn't bear it."

She extended both wrists, holding them upward in supplication. "I'm yours, Max. I don't want to ever be anything else. I'll never take them off unless you ask me to."

He leaned forward, finding her lips in the sweetest of kisses. "Good, because I'm never going to ask."

CHAPTER 12

HOLLY awoke in the middle of the night shivering, and the ache in her lower side had intensified to a fiery pain that wasn't alleviated by movement. Ryan lay sleeping beside her, but no one was on her other side. Adam and Ethan had evidently taken to their own beds instead of crashing in the common bedroom tonight.

She pushed to the vacant side, careful not to awaken Ryan. Her feet hit the cold floor and she shivered as another chill overtook her. Fire splintered through her side and she hunched over, grabbing for the edge of the bed to steady herself. Nausea welled in her throat and she swallowed hard against the urge to vomit.

She managed to stagger into the kitchen, and she opened the medicine cabinet to get some ibuprofen. After shaking out four pills, she returned the bottle and started toward the cabinet for a glass.

Pain assaulted her, spearing through her, robbing her of breath. She fell, hitting the floor with a thud, driving the air from her lungs in a painful rush. She lay there, balled into a fetal position, afraid to move because the pain was so horrific.

Something was terribly, terribly wrong.

"Ryan," she called weakly. "Adam? Ethan?"

Darkness hovered on the fringes. She fought unconsciousness as the pain intensified. She heard a distant sound, tried to call out again, but the blackness swirled until she was dizzy with it.

RYAN awoke, a frown turning his lips downward. It was automatic to reach for Holly, a habit he hadn't broken in over thirty years. But she wasn't there. Something had awakened him. His name. He could swear he'd heard her call.

Throwing aside the covers, he hurried out of bed

and into the hall. No lights were on in the house and it was silent. The fire had long since died out in the living room and only a few glowing embers remained.

"Holly?" he called.

Something like dread pitted his stomach and clutched at his throat. He hadn't checked his brothers' bedrooms because he'd just known that wasn't where she was. After surveying the living room, he walked toward the kitchen and damn near tripped over her before he'd gotten far.

His heart bottomed out. He dropped to his knees, yelling her name hoarsely. She was in a tiny ball, knees drawn up as if she were in unimaginable pain. Her skin was hot and dry to the touch. He immediately felt for a pulse, relieved to find a steady rhythm against his fingers.

"Adam! Ethan!" he roared. "Get in here!"

Gently, he collected Holly in his arms, unsure of what to do. He only knew he wasn't leaving her lying on the cold floor.

Not ten seconds later, his brothers ran down the hall and appeared in the kitchen.

"What happened?" Adam barked.

Ethan crowded into Ryan, his hands going to

Holly's face and then her neck, frantic, just as Ryan had been to feel the reassuring pulse pattern.

"What's wrong with her?" Ethan demanded.

"I woke up when I thought I heard her call for me. She was gone and so I got up and found her on the floor," Ryan said grimly. "Get the keys. We have to get her to the hospital."

His words sent his brothers in different directions. Ethan grabbed a blanket and tossed it over her as Ryan headed for the door. Adam sprinted toward the bedroom and returned a moment later, dressed and holding the keys to the SUV.

"Get me some damn clothes," Ryan bit out in Ethan's direction. "You can change on the way and I'll get dressed when we get there."

He wasn't about to let Holly go long enough to rectify his current mode of undress.

FOUR hours later, the three brothers paced around the waiting room, edgy, silent, worried sick. The doors burst open and their children rushed in, their faces white, eyes filled with fear.

Adam immediately went into protective mode. His

wife was in surgery and he was scared out of his mind, but he didn't want his sons and his daughter to be as afraid as he was.

"Daddy," Callie said, rushing into his arms. "What's wrong with Mama? What happened?"

Adam crushed her to him and held on a long moment while his sons went to stand by their other two dads. Lily stood back with Max, but she looked no less concerned than everyone else.

Adam pulled away from Callie and motioned his brood into one of the smaller side rooms usually reserved for the doctor to speak to the family. When everyone was pushed inside, he took a deep breath and glanced over at his brothers.

"Your mother is in surgery."

Dillon looked crushed. Michael's lips drew into a grim line, and Seth looked utterly baffled, as if he couldn't quite grasp it all.

Callie's eyes filled with tears and Max wrapped a supportive arm around her.

"What's wrong?" Dillon croaked out, his voice choked with fear.

"Appendicitis," Ethan said quietly. "They believe it may have already ruptured. They didn't waste a lot of time going in. We won't know more until the doctor comes out of surgery."

No one looked as though they had any idea what to say or do. They stood numbly, staring at one another, helpless anxiety reflected in their gazes. If Holly were here, she'd take charge. She'd soothe everyone. Do what she did best. Love with all her heart and warm the entire world inside and out.

Adam sank into his chair, his legs no longer able to hold him up. Callie immediately wrapped her arms around him, hugging him tightly. "She'll be all right, Daddy," she whispered fiercely. "She loves you all too much to go down. She'll probably be back on her feet in no time. You know she wouldn't miss Christmas for the world."

Adam smiled faintly, amused by the fact that his precious daughter was the one providing comfort for him. It was his job to protect his children. His wife. Only now his sons and his daughter were gathered around, offering their support to him and his brothers.

All through the rest of the night, they sat in grim silence, and the realization of just how important a role Holly played in their family was outlined in stark reality. She was the very center. The heart and soul. The one around whom the rest of the family revolved.

Every heart. Every child. Every man. They all loved her with a fierceness that couldn't be described, only felt.

She was everything to this family, and Adam didn't even want to contemplate how they would survive without her. She was their strength. Their light. The glue that held them all together.

He could see her in every one of his children. Callie's infectious smile. Her exuberance for life. Her kindness and gentleness. Her fierce stubbornness and her endless capacity for love and her undying loyalty to those she loved.

Seth's steadfastness. His quiet strength. His resilience. Michael's intelligence. His work ethic. His quiet spirit. The way Dillon loved with all his heart and soul. Just like Holly.

"Daddy?" Callie whispered. "She'll be okay."

It wasn't posed as a question but he could hear the uncertainty in his daughter's voice. She was trying to offer him the encouragement she so desperately needed herself.

Adam drew her into a hug. "Yes, baby. Your mother's going to be fine. She's a fighter through and through. She's been down before, much worse than this, and she refused to stay down."

Just then the doctor came into the small room and everyone looked up, the sudden silence tense and forbidding. Tension coiled and snaked through the room. Dread mounted and everyone leaned forward, eager to hear what the doctor would say.

"Mrs. Colter is out of surgery," the doctor began.

Not able to contain himself another moment, Adam shot to his feet, but Ethan beat him to the doctor.

"How is she?" Ethan demanded. "Will she be all right? When can we see her?"

The surgeon held up a placating hand. "She'll be fine. She'll make a full recovery. We were able to remove her appendix before it burst. I'll want her to stay in the hospital a day or two so I can be certain there's no infection or leakage, but if all goes well she'll be home before Christmas."

The relief in the room was palpable. Adam's shoulders sagged and his eyes burned with sudden tears. Holly was his life. His entire life. And, oh God, he couldn't lose her.

Dillon's arm went around him and Adam turned, hugging his son fiercely as the others comforted one another.

"When can we see her?" Ethan asked hoarsely.

The doctor eyed the room full of people with doubt. "You can't all see her. One of you can go in when she gets out of recovery."

Ryan scowled. "Hell no. We can manage three, but we're going in to see her."

The doctor cleared his throat. "It's customary for a spouse to have access. The rest of the family must wait until she's in a room."

"We *are* her damn husbands," Ryan snarled. He jabbed his thumb into his chest and then jerked it over his shoulder to point at Ethan and Adam.

The doctor's brows lifted and he went silent. He fiddled with his clipboard and uneasily fidgeted. "Uh, well, there isn't a precedent for this. Perhaps you should take it up with the nurse in charge."

After saying that, the doctor beat a hasty retreat, muttering under his breath as he went.

Ryan turned back to Adam and Ethan. "Let's go. They'll let us in or I'll tear this damn place apart."

Ethan chuckled, the tension escaping in a rush. "You don't have a good track record with hospitals, man." He turned to Adam. "Remember when his cranky ass was shot and he pissed off every nurse and doctor in the ER and on the floor until they put him in the same room as Holly?"

Adam smiled but his heart clutched at that long-ago memory. At the moment he knew he'd be every bit as forceful as Ryan if they dared to keep him away from his wife.

CHAPTER 13

IT was as if time had stopped and for the moment Christmas had been suspended into a nebulous cloud that floated above the Colter family. Everyone refused to even contemplate the holiday without Holly at home, surrounded by her family.

She was, as Adam had asserted, the very center, the heart and soul of her husbands and children.

Holly sat in the hospital bed, her fingers gripping the sheet as she considered her options. With Christmas just a few days away, the very last thing she wanted was to be stuck in a hospital room when she could be at home, surrounded by the family she so dearly loved.

"I'm not asking, Dr. Hollister," she said calmly, because she'd long ago discovered that calm was hard to argue with. "I'd like to be discharged today. I understand your concerns, and I'll heed your instructions to the letter, but I would recover more rapidly in my own home."

"Nothing like throwing me to the wolves," the doctor said dryly. "Those husbands of yours will kick my ass if I let you walk out of here before *they* believe it's time. Hard to remember who has the medical degree here."

The light sarcasm in his voice made Holly grin. Dr. Hollister had been Holly's physician for years. He was well acquainted with her unusual situation, just as he was very well acquainted with her husbands' huge protective streak when it came to her.

"I want to be home for Christmas," she said, an ache in her voice that was more pronounced than any residual pain from her surgery. "It's going to be so wonderful this year. And I'm cooking!"

Dr. Hollister stared at her over his glasses and tactfully cleared his throat. "Well, maybe it's best if you aren't puttering around a kitchen quite yet."

Holly snorted. "You've listened to far too many stories about my lack of ability in the kitchen. My daughter-in-law is a dream cook, and she's taught me how to make the most awesome holiday dinner." Her smile softened wistfully. "All my babies are going to be home this year. That hasn't happened in so long. We always have most, but not everyone. No way I'm going to miss that."

Dr. Hollister smiled indulgently. "I'm going to let you go, Holly. I don't fool myself into thinking that if I said no you'd actually listen to me. But I want you to follow my care instructions to the letter, and don't think I won't outline them in great detail to your husbands."

She scowled at him. "I'm not staying in bed twenty-four/seven. Just so you know. Don't even hint to my husbands that this is part of your care plan."

He chuckled and shook his head. "What I'm going to tell them is that you are to resume normal activities with caution and that you are to rest perhaps more than usual until you're feeling more yourself again. I want you to take your medications and I want you to listen to your body, Holly. I'm serious about this. If it's telling you to slow down and rest, then do it. You don't want to end up back in the hospital, I assume?"

She shook her head vigorously.

"Then follow my instructions and we'll all be happy. Your husbands included."

"Okay, okay," she grumbled. "How soon can you have me discharged?"

He sighed. "One-track mind you have. Give me an hour, okay? I need to give the nurse my report and write your scripts. She'll be down to set you loose as soon as I'm done. Happy?"

She beamed at him. "Thanks, Pete. You know I appreciate you."

He rolled his eyes. "You only appreciate me when you're bending me to your will." He leaned over to give her a kiss on the cheek. "Take care of yourself, okay? I'll want to see you again in a week. If you don't want to drive up to the city, I'll be happy to come out on a Saturday."

Holly snagged his hand and squeezed. Over the years, Pete Hollister had become a family friend. During that terrible time when she'd been attacked and then had discovered her pregnancy, he'd been a rock. And because she'd trusted him, she'd continued to seek his medical care in the years afterward. She and her husbands had donated a large sum of money to fund his clinic for those who couldn't afford healthcare and had no insurance, and as a result he felt deep loyalty to the Colters. It was nothing for him to drop everything and make the trip to Clyde if one of them needed care beyond what the general practitioner in Clyde provided. And, well, he didn't seem to trust others to care for the Colters. He'd sort of adopted them, and while he gave her husbands grief over being so protective of *her*, he was just as protective of the Colters as a whole.

"Thanks, Pete," she said again. "I hope you have a merry Christmas."

"Not seeing you in my hospital again will make my holidays go a lot better."

Holly smiled and nodded and then sank back onto the pillows behind her as the doctor left the room. A few moments later, the door swung open again and her husbands stalked in, suspicious looks on their faces.

"I thought you said Pete wasn't coming by until later." Ryan said with a scowl. "We just passed him in the hall and it looked like he'd just come out of your room."

Holly put her hands over her lap and smiled serenely. "He did."

Adam sighed. "Let me guess. You strong-armed

him into letting you go and you sent us out on a fool's errand so we wouldn't be here to disagree."

She grinned because she wasn't about to try and deny it. Her husbands knew her far too well.

"For God's sake," Ethan grumbled as he sat on the edge of the bed next to her. "Do you even want what we brought back for you?"

"Yes! I'm starving," she said, pouncing on the bag Ethan held out.

"Do you even have time to eat?" Adam drawled. "Or will you be pushed out of here in the next fifteen minutes?"

She made a face. "I have an hour at least."

Ryan's eyes went heavenward and he shook his head in resignation.

"I want to go home," she said stubbornly. "I'm not spending Christmas in the hospital."

To emphasize her statement, she raised her arms and crossed them over her chest. She thrust out her chin in a gesture of defiance and sent them a mutinous glare.

Ryan leaned down and kissed her furrowed brow. "We worry about you. You know that."

She went completely soft and she turned her face up to stare into those intense blue eyes so like Callie's.

"I know you do and I love you for it. But if you want what's best for me? That's to go home and be surrounded by my husbands and my children and to spend Christmas there. Not here. I can rest much easier there, and I've already promised Pete I wouldn't overdo it. He's going to give you a list of dos and don'ts so that he'll be sure you enforce them."

"I've always liked that man," Adam said approvingly.

Holly snorted. "You just like him because he sides with you."

Ethan grinned beside her and tugged her hand into his. "You know it."

"I'm ready to be home," she said softly. "There's no other place I'd rather be."

"And we want you there," Adam said, emotion knotting his throat. "You gave us a scare, baby."

Ryan stroked her cheek with his palm and then lowered his lips to hers. "Don't do that again."

She smiled. "I'll try my best not to end up in the hospital ever again."

"That's what you said the last time," Ethan grumbled.

Knowing her food was getting cold, she gestured for the portable tray and Adam wheeled it over to the bed, sliding the arm over her lap so she'd have a place to eat.

While she dug into the food, Ethan made phone calls to the boys and to Callie to let them know she was coming home that day.

Holly smiled in anticipation because she knew they'd all be waiting. All gathered in her home, just where she liked them.

CHAPTER 14

SETH, Michael, and Dillon stood across the room from the couch where Lily lay sound asleep, and they smiled. She was curled on her side, head nestled on one of the cushions.

They were all tired. The last few days had been nerve-racking as they'd waited for their mother to be released from the hospital. Now that she was finally home, the dads had banished all the children to their own homes to get some much-needed rest.

"This pregnancy seems to be kicking her ass," Seth said in a low voice. "Even before the thing with Mom, I mean. I'm as nervous as hell over this. I don't want her getting so beat down that she feels even for a moment like she did with Rose."

Dillon's expression grew fierce. "That ain't going to happen. I don't care if I have to sell the damn pub or have Callie take it over so I can spend every waking moment with Lily. I don't want her to *ever* feel that kind of despair again."

"I second that," Michael said somberly. "She's had a hard time coming to grips with this. I don't think she was ready. Hell, I'm not even sure how she managed to get pregnant. I know birth control isn't foolproof but it still has a pretty damn good success rate."

"No sense belaboring that point now," Seth said. "What's important is how we make her feel from this point forward. I don't want her to doubt, even for a moment, our commitment to her and our child. I want her to go into the delivery room knowing that she has absolutely nothing to worry about this time."

Dillon nodded his agreement. His jaw was set into a fierce line and Seth knew he was probably already planning the next seven months and beyond. It wouldn't surprise Seth whatsoever if Dillon did let the management of the pub go. However, he doubted Max would ever allow Callie to take over the running of it full-time, and in this instance Seth would fully support his brother-in-law. Callie didn't need to be stuck behind the damn bar every night, nor did she need to be dragging home at all hours of the morning.

He'd had his doubts about Max being the dominant force in his relationship with Callie. It had pissed him off, truth be told. But Max adored and worshipped Callie, and it was hard to find fault with the hard-ass when he would cut off his right arm before ever allowing any harm to come to Callie.

"Has she been sick in the mornings?" Michael asked.

Michael often left early, before everyone else was out of bed, so he wasn't around when Lily began her day. His workday started early at his veterinary clinic but he always made it a point to be home by the afternoon. It was a schedule they worked out together. Dillon, more often than not, worked evenings at the pub when things were busier. Callie covered some nights for him so he wasn't always away from home. Seth could be called out at literally any hour of the day or night. His traditional hours were eight to five, but it was rare for him to stick to that schedule. As sheriff he was on call twenty-four hours a day, seven days a week, rain or shine, holiday or not.

But they'd arranged it so that someone was always home with Lily, and now Seth was more grateful than ever that they'd taken those steps.

Dillon grimaced. "Some, yeah. The problem is that she's been sick at all intervals of the day."

Seth nodded. "Smells seem to do her in more than anything. Painting's been hard for her in the past few days because the paint nauseates her."

"She walked by the cat litter yesterday and had to run for the bathroom to puke her guts up," Dillon said wryly.

Michael frowned. "What the hell is she doing near the cat litter anyway? She's not supposed to be changing litter when she's pregnant. I swear I'm going to get rid of that damn cat."

Seth snorted in amusement. As if Michael would ever get rid of Lily's precious cat. The stray had been dumped at the clinic on a day when Lily had been helping Michael, and she'd given Michael puppy dog eyes, and voilà, the cat found a new home. With them. And it had been with them ever since.

"I didn't say she *changed* the cat litter," Dillon said with a scowl. "I said she walked *by* it. As in, by the mudroom where the litter is. The cat had just taken a dump and it did Lily in."

So deep were they in their discussion that they hadn't realized that Lily had awakened. Only when she moved to sit up did Seth notice.

Her eyes gleamed with amusement and a soft smile curved her lips. She leaned her elbow on the arm of the couch and rested her face in her palm as she stared at her husbands.

"If you could only hear yourselves," she teased. "Like a bunch of mother hens."

Dillon moved toward the couch until he loomed over her. "I highly doubt a mother hen thinks how much she'd like to see you naked right about now."

She arched one dark brow and then her smile broadened.

"Or what kind of vulgar, indecent things she'd like to do to you," Michael offered as he went to sit beside her on the couch.

She laughed and then her gaze found Seth's. "And you? Not going to add your two cents?"

His let his gaze stroke silkily over her until she was well aware of just what occupied his thoughts. "My brothers talk too damn much. While they're *telling* you what they want to do to you, I'm going to be showing you."

To prove his point, he pushed forward, pulled her

to her feet before Dillon or Michael could react, and swept her into his arms, heading for the bedroom.

She laughed out loud at the what-the-fuck looks on his brothers' faces and it hit Seth right in the gut. She sounded and looked so damn beautiful. She looked happy. Her eyes were full of joy and warmth. The worry was gone, even if the signs of her fatigue were still etched in the lines of her face.

He pressed his lips to her forehead and closed his eyes as they entered the bedroom. How much had his life changed over the last year and a half? Not only had he found the love of his life in Lily, but he was closer than ever to his family. Surrounded by his brothers, his sister, and his mom and dads.

Now his child would grow up sheltered by the love and support of his family. The same love he and his siblings had been given as children.

"Seth, are you all right?" Lily asked softly.

He refocused his attention to see Lily staring up at him, her blue eyes shadowed with worry. Then he smiled. He honest to God wanted to spin her around in a dozen circles and do something crazy like let out a series of whoops, but it wasn't the smartest thing to do with a pregnant woman who had a queasy stomach.

"Yeah," he said huskily. "I'm just so damn happy."

He laid her on the bed with a gentle bounce. Dillon and Michael stood to the side as if waiting for him to finish his piece. Hell, what else was there to say? How could you possibly put words to indescribable joy?

"I love you," he said. "I hope you know that."

The worry faded, replaced by warmth and answering love. "I love you too, Seth. I hope you know I trust you." She moved her head to include his brothers in her gaze. "I trust all of you. I know you'll help me through the pregnancy and afterward. Our child will be so loved. I don't doubt that even for a moment."

"That's good," Michael said as he moved onto the bed beside her. He lay on his side, head propped in his palm as he gazed down at her. He put his hand over her belly, cupping protectively as if he were sending a silent message, a pledge of protection. And love.

"Make love to me," she whispered, in turn seeking each of her husbands' gazes. "Show me your love."

Seth put both hands on the bed and lowered himself until their faces were just an inch apart and her lips delectably close. "If I have my way, you'll know our love every single day for the rest of our lives."

* * *

MAX slipped from the warmth of his bed, reluctant to leave Callie. She was exhausted and worn down both physically and emotionally, and she'd only just gotten over her bout with strep throat. Having her mother in the hospital and seeing how frightened her fathers had been had shaken Callie to the core.

Now that Holly was back home, the family breathed easier. The collective sigh of the entire town could be heard through the mountain air. Holly Colter was home. All was well.

But Max was driven to make Christmas extra special. More so than it would already be. He knew the Colters, and especially Holly, were thrilled to have all their children home for the holidays.

He and Callie had traveled last Christmas. He'd taken her to Paris and London, where they'd marveled at the Christmas lights and festivities, and then they'd gone on to Germany, where they'd spent days just absorbing the atmosphere.

Callie had been born a free spirit. It was how he'd met her. She'd been backpacking in Greece and he'd been there for a short vacation of his own. As soon as he'd laid eyes on her, he'd known that she would alter his life forever.

He hadn't reacted well. It was shame he'd forever live with. He'd very nearly messed up the best thing that had ever happened to him, but thank God for Callie's forgiving spirit because he'd messed up not once, but twice.

Yes, he and Callie both liked to roam. They were restless and eager to explore new places. But one thing he'd realized in the time he and Callie had been married was that she belonged here. With her family. On this mountain. In her meadow, the place where she'd been born. Callie's Meadow.

And oddly, he found himself craving the return to the warm embrace of the Colter family when he and Callie were away. It had been he who'd suggested that they spend this Christmas with family. Not just Callie's family anymore, but his own. And now Lauren's.

He crept from the bedroom, knowing that if he wanted to get done what he'd planned, it would take care and precision. But most of all, time. Time that was fast running out as Christmas approached.

When he reached the office in the corner of the downstairs level, just off the living room, he picked up the phone and began making calls. Money was no object. The work would have to be done at night. By the time he was finished, he was short a hefty amount of cash but he was satisfied that he'd been assured that what he wanted would be done.

Now, however, he needed to go make damn sure that Callie's dads didn't end up shooting someone for trespassing in the dead of night.

If he hurried, he could make it back in time to cook breakfast for his girls. He smiled as the word simmered in his mind. His girls. The woman he loved more than anything and his baby sister. Both here and safe with him. Family.

He went for his coat, grabbed the keys to the Range Rover, and headed out the door. Normally he'd make the walk across the meadow to the Colters' cabin, but he wanted to make it back before Callie and Lauren got up.

A few minutes later, he pulled up to the Colters' cabin and slid out of the car. He was almost to the door when it opened and Ethan called out a greeting.

"Morning, Max. What brings you out so early?"

Max took the extended hand and shook it before following Ethan inside, where it was a good deal warmer. Already a fire blazed in the big stone hearth and the room was alive with the twinkling Christmas lights strung from the tree and along the mantel.

It just felt like home in this big, cozy cabin that had once housed hunters when the Colters had operated a guide service for elk hunting.

"How is Holly?" Max asked.

Ethan was quiet for a moment and his hand shook as he raised the cup of coffee he was holding to his lips. After he took a sip, he turned his gaze on Max. "She's doing better. She's happy to be home. She doesn't like to be away for long and being in the hospital was driving her crazy."

"I bet," Max replied. "I'm glad she's home, and I know Callie is super relieved."

"Yeah, we all are," Ethan said quietly. "She scared the hell out of us. It's a sobering wake-up call when you realize just how close you come to losing someone or how easily they can slip away."

But Max knew. He knew all too well because he'd come so damn close to losing Callie that it still hurt him to think about it.

Adam walked into the living room, his head rearing back in surprise when he saw Max standing there.

"Anything the matter, son?" Adam asked.

Max was a grown man, but it still gave him a

ridiculous thrill when Adam called him son. It made him feel included. Like another of the Colter brothers. His place certainly hadn't always been assured in this family. He was lucky Callie's dads and brothers hadn't wiped the earth with him and ripped his nuts off. It certainly wasn't because they hadn't wanted to.

But now there was warmth and acceptance, and Max soaked it in. With the passing of his mother, he and Lauren had been left alone in the world. Having the Colters was something he treasured greatly, and he'd go to any lengths to protect what he now considered his. They had his loyalty and his love.

"No, not at all," Max said. "I wanted to see how Holly was doing so I could let Callie know when she gets up. She was pretty tired and I wanted to let her sleep, but I know the minute she wakes up, she's going to be worried about her mama."

"That's nice of you," Ethan said. "I know Holly will appreciate your concern. We all do."

Max glanced at both men. "I also wanted to discuss something with you. A little surprise I have in mind for the women in the family."

At the mention of the women, Max had Adam's and Ethan's undivided attention. One thing he'd quickly learned in the two years he'd known this family was that the Colters treasured their women. They pampered them, spoiled them, and loved them beyond measure.

"What's your plan, and do you need our help?" Adam asked.

Max smiled. "I won't need your help, except in keeping the secret, of course. I will, however, need to make you aware that for the next several nights, you're going to have a crew crawling all over Callie's Meadow. I've made sure they'll be coming late and leaving before dawn. Where I have it planned isn't easily visible from the road so I think we'll be safe. Plus, I know Holly won't be getting out and about, and if Callie's going to come over, I'll make damn sure I drive her myself."

Ethan grinned. "How well you know us. No, Holly won't be lifting so much as a damn finger between now and Christmas so you certainly won't have to worry about her finding out."

"Okay, so tell us exactly what you're doing," Adam said.

Max smiled and then related everything he'd just spent the last hour setting up over the phone. When he was done, both Ethan and Adam were smiling broadly. Adam slapped him on the back.

"They're going to love it."

CHAPTER 15

"DO you remember our first Christmas together?" Holly asked softly.

She was sitting on the couch, blanket hugged up all around her. Only her hands stuck out, clutching the cup of hot chocolate that Ryan had given her moments before.

The fire roared in the hearth and outside snow was falling at a steady pace. If she was feeling better, it would have been a wonderful day to get the sleigh and play. Her husbands would have heart attacks if she even suggested stepping foot outdoors.

Adam was sitting next to her while Ethan was on

her other side. Ryan stood by the hearth, poking at one of the logs to stoke the flames.

Ethan's hand went to her head, smoothing back her hair, his smile gentle and full of love. His eyes had a faraway look of remembrance.

"It was the best Christmas ever," Ethan said.

Emotion glimmered in Ryan's eyes as he settled into an armchair across from the couch. "Seth was just a baby and we were still reeling and so damn grateful to have you back in our lives."

Adam's arm tightened around Holly. A tremor raced up his body and she turned, smiling tenderly at him. He still hated the mention of the time they'd spent apart. He hated remembering the fear that they'd lost her, that she wasn't coming back.

But she'd known. There was never a question that she'd make her way back home to the men who loved her.

"So many Christmases since then," she said, her voice aching at the memories. "But you know what? I have a feeling this will be the best yet."

Ethan smiled indulgently. "You say that every year."

She pulled a face. "I didn't say that last year when

Callie and Max were in Europe. I hated that they were gone."

"This year will be special," Ryan said. "It'll be nice to have our children home. All of them."

Holly's eyes glittered with tears that she didn't try to hide. Her life was so full and wonderful. Each and every day. How many people could say that? How many people could say they were loved as Holly was loved?

She was surrounded by it. It enveloped her. Her husbands, her children. Those who'd joined the family. Max and Lauren. And Lily. Sweet, fragile Lily who'd turned her boys' lives upside down.

"If you start crying, you're going to hurt," Adam said gruffly. "Doc said you'd be sore for a few days."

"You just hate to see me cry," she teased.

"That too."

He kissed the side of her head. "I love you, you know."

Her smile broadened. "Yeah, I know."

She turned back to include Ryan and Ethan in her view.

"I think we should take a trip after Christmas."

Ryan's brows drew together and Ethan shot her a

puzzled look. She couldn't blame them. She was happiest when she was right here in her own home, surrounded by the people she loved. Callie was the one with wanderlust, always going, wanting to go, waiting for that next adventure.

"What kind of trip?" Adam asked hesitantly.

"Oh, I don't know. Maybe someplace warm. Hawaii or some tropical island somewhere. Someplace private, maybe a private beach where we could just lounge and make love and stay naked all week if we wanted."

Ethan blinked. "Well, hell."

"I vote you stay naked," Ryan drawled. "Maybe the rest of us will at least wear swim trunks, but you, sweetheart, I'd love to keep naked for as long as possible."

Her heart fluttered and went soft. After all these years, they still thought she was the most beautiful woman in the world. They still desired her. Still wanted her. That had never changed, never slowed. Their love had only gotten better and stronger with age.

"We're as young as we want to be," she said.

Adam lifted a brow at that. "Are you feeling your years, baby? Because I have to say that you damn sure don't look like a woman in her fifties."

She blushed to her toes at the hungry look in his eyes. "I was just reminding myself that age is just a number. It's all in how you feel, and you know what I feel?"

"What?"

The question came from all three men.

She smiled and kept smiling, the grin growing bigger until her cheeks hurt. "I feel loved, and as long as I feel as loved as I do, I'll stay young forever. This whole episode made me realize that there's still a lot I want to do, and I don't want to miss out on anything. Maybe after we take a trip we can get together with Max and Callie. Plan a family trip for us all. Us, Max and Callie. Even Lauren. Seth, Michael, Dillon, and Lily. Think how much fun it would be to take a big family vacation. We haven't done that since the children were young."

Ryan's eyes went soft. "We'll take you wherever you want to go, sweetheart. I can't imagine a better time than one spent with my family. But first we'll take our trip. Just us, a beach, and a sunset somewhere."

"Gets my vote," Ethan said.

Adam's eyes gleamed with mischief as he stared at Holly. "Just think how easy it'll be to pack. You won't even have to bring a suitcase."

Her brows puckered up as she glanced questioningly up at him.

He leaned over and kissed away the lines on her forehead. "You don't have to pack if you're going to stay naked for the entire time, and that damn sure gets my vote."

CHAPTER 16

LILY sat on the edge of her bed, her bottom lip firmly between her teeth as she stared sightlessly toward the closet. Anxiety ate a hole in her stomach. It was Christmas Eve. They were due at her in laws' soon—they should have already left.

They'd decided to tell the entire family tonight. At dinner. A surprise. A wonderful Christmas present.

She closed her eyes. She wasn't sure she was prepared. She almost wished she would have gone a quieter route. Told Holly and Callie first. Then maybe the dads. Then she wouldn't have to face everyone at once.

But neither did she want to deprive her husbands of their special moment. They were over the moon. Cautious. Worried about her. But over the moon ecstatic at the thought of having a child. She knew they wanted several. As many as she was comfortable having.

And maybe she did too. She loved the Colter family. Loved everything about them. She wanted it for *her* family. Her husbands. Her children.

If only she could move past this paralyzing fear that gripped her every time she dwelled more than a moment on the growing life inside her.

"Lily?"

She glanced up to see Dillon standing at the door. His stance told her he'd been standing there awhile. Watching her. Probably worrying.

He walked in without saying anything further and slid onto the bed next to her so that their thighs were touching.

"Everything okay?"

She nodded, hesitated a moment, and then sighed. "I'm just nervous. Maybe a little scared. I know everyone will be happy, but they'll be worried too. I'm afraid they won't want to be too excited because they won't know how well I'm taking it. I don't want to suck the joy out of this moment for them like I did with you."

Dillon frowned and turned more fully toward her so he could capture her with his glare. "You did *not* ruin the moment for me. You've got to cut yourself some slack, Lily. You took a hit. You weren't expecting to become pregnant. It wasn't something we planned. Under the circumstances, I think you handled it quite well."

She smiled wanly. "Thanks for saying that."

He caught her hand and squeezed. "Mom and the dads are going to be overjoyed. Of course they're going to worry about you. They love you. They know what you've been through. But they'll know when you tell them. They'll be able to see it in your eyes. Nothing will ruin that moment for them. Learning at Christmas that they're going to have their first grandchild will be a memory they'll hold forever. And you're the one who'll give that to them."

She sucked in a breath. "I know it's stupid for me to be afraid and nervous. I mean, I love them so much and I know they love me. They've shown me nothing but support and caring. I couldn't have ever asked for a better family. I guess I just don't want to let anyone down. Especially myself and our baby."

Dillon touched her cheek and then leaned in to kiss her softly on the lips. "Never that, Lily. You won't disappoint them or us. We couldn't be prouder of you."

She dove into his arms, wrapping herself around him to hug him tight. He curled his arms around her and held her just as tightly.

He smoothed her hair and then murmured close to her ear, "What do you say we go have the best Christmas Eve this family's ever seen?"

CHAPTER 17

CHRISTMAS Eve was always a big event in the Colter household. Not that Christmas Day was completely overlooked, but Christmas Eve was full of excitement. It was when the family gathered, drank hot chocolate in front of the fire, and laughed and loved as they celebrated another year.

Christmas Day they would sleep in, eat breakfast in their pajamas, open presents, and then everyone would watch the Christmas parades and football until they ate a midafternoon Christmas dinner.

This Christmas Eve, just as the sun went down, bathing the fresh covering of snow in the first pale shadows of dusk, the Colters and Wilders gathered at the Colter cabin.

Presents were piled around the tree and spilled onto the hearth. The living room was aglow with twinkling lights and the sounds of laughter and happiness.

Holly sat at the end of the couch, propped with pillows and fussed over endlessly by her husbands and children alike. Adam and Ryan disappeared frequently into the kitchen along with Dillon as they cooked the Christmas Eve feast.

And what a feast it was.

The table had been extended over the years, leaves added as the family grew in number. As they gathered at the table, Lily smiled a soft, secret smile, imagining her own addition to the Colter family who would arrive a few months down the road.

This was her child's future. This family. This wonderful, loving group of people who had hearts as big as the Rocky Mountains.

She was going to be okay. Her child was going to be okay.

She could be happy. Fear uncoiled its tight grip around her heart and slid away, replaced by peace and overwhelming joy. And gratitude. For this second chance—at love, at a life, to have another child to love and cherish.

She glanced at her husbands as they sat down, her heart swelling with love and excitement. This was her moment. Her time to shine. After so long in the shadows, afraid to step into the sun, she was ready to burst out, throw her arms wide, and turn her face up to the wonder of heaven and glory in God's mercy and grace.

Dillon reached underneath the table to squeeze her hand. Then Seth reached for her other hand, his fingers laced tightly with hers. Across the table, Michael met her gaze and smiled, his eyes suspiciously bright. It was time.

Lily took in a deep breath to steady her nerves. It wasn't that she had doubts—she didn't. But she knew their news would concern her parents-in-law. They all knew of her past tragedy. They constantly surrounded her with love and unconditional support. She didn't want them to worry that she'd fall apart. This family made her strong. With them behind her, she could do anything.

She very carefully disentangled her hands from her husbands' and then rose, tall and strong, and stared down the table at the rest of the family, who were seated.

Conversation died and the room went silent. All eyes were on Lily as if they realized that something big was about to happen. Holly's eyes flashed with concern and Lily saw her reach for Ethan's hand automatically.

Lily smiled, unsure whether she'd even be able to get this out without becoming a blubbering mess. Her eyes already stung and she fought to know just how to begin.

Then beside her, Seth stood, reaching for her hand. He gave her a reassuring smile, full of love and strength—his strength that he was lending her.

Dillon rose on her other side and took her hand as Seth had. Then Michael also stood.

Lily didn't even try to control the tears that slid silently down her cheeks. Her smile was so wide that no one could possibly confuse her tears for sadness or grief.

Confident in her husbands' love and support, she faced the rest of the table once more.

"We have something special to share with you," she said softly. It was hard to talk when her smile was so big and tears streamed endlessly down her cheeks.

Then she looked pointedly at the end of the table where the older generation of Colters sat.

"You're going to have a grandchild. I'm pregnant."

A series of gasps flew around the table. Concern immediately flashed in the eyes of the Colters, but so did utter happiness and excitement.

Tears filled Holly's eyes. Callie wiped at her own eyes as she glanced back at Lily. Lauren smiled but her smile was wistful, almost poignant, as if it reflected her own wishes and dreams.

And the dads' reactions ranged from shock to satisfaction.

The silence abruptly ended as everyone reacted at the same moment. Whoops went up. Cheers erupted. A barrage of congratulations flew. Despite her husbands' attempts to keep her seated, Holly jumped from her chair and dashed around to where Lily stood.

She enfolded her daughter-in-law in her arms and whispered in her ear, "Oh my baby, I'm so very happy for you. You know it'll be all right this time."

Lily clung to her mother-in-law, closing her eyes as emotion knotted her throat. There were so many differing feelings to sort through. But best was this hug. This hug told her that she was loved and supported unconditionally. That her child would have the best the world could offer him or her. That her child would grow up in a family as strong and enduring as time itself.

"I do know," she whispered back. "I'm okay. I'm more than okay."

Holly pulled away and suddenly the dads were there, pulling her into big, bone-crushing hugs. Seth, Michael, and Dillon all got slaps on the back, hugs, handshakes.

Callie and Lauren crowded in and hugged Lily next, and Lily absorbed the moment, so very different from her first pregnancy, when she'd been so alone and isolated. This time would be different. This time she was *loved*.

Max came forward to hug her. He kissed her wet cheek and then shook the hands of Seth, Michael, and Dillon. Everyone was talking at once. Exclaiming. Such happy sounds. Laughter. Joy. It was a balm to a soul that had long suffered the agony of silence.

Adam cleared his throat to get everyone's attention, and to Lily's surprise, tears gleamed in his eyes. He looked shaky. Happy. A little unbalanced. He kept staring at his sons with such love in his eyes that Lily felt the answering sting of tears once more.

Seth wrapped his arm around her and pulled her close as Adam motioned for quiet.

"That's the best damn news I've had, apart from your mother being okay after she gave us such a fright." His expression grew more serious and he stared at Lily, singling her out. "Lily, honey, I just want you to know that we're all going to be here for you. You never doubt that for a moment. You and our grandchild will be loved and cherished and covered up with support, so much so you'll probably want to tell us all to buzz off."

Laughter filled the room and Lily smiled through the ache of tears.

He reached for his glass, wiped absently at his eyes, and then faced his family again. He held up his glass and enveloped Lily and his sons in the warmth of his gaze. "To the first Colter grandchild. May he or she grow up surrounded by love. May he or she grow up to become as wonderful as my own children are. And may he or she have the resiliency and indomitable spirit of his mother."

"Hear, hear."

The soft murmurs of agreement broke Lily. She could no longer hold back the sobs that welled in her throat.

"What would I do without all of you?" she asked tearfully. "No one has ever been as protected and loved as I have. My baby will be the luckiest child in the world."

"And the most spoiled," Callie said dryly.

Laughter met her declaration. Holly let out a humph. "If I can't spoil my grandchildren, who can I spoil?"

"Sit, everyone," Adam said, motioning everyone down. "Let's eat before the food gets cold."

Dishes were passed around. Chatter buzzed in Lily's ears. Questions flew. There was already the question of names. So much that she hadn't allowed herself to contemplate yet.

It felt good to have it out in the open. Real. Excitement squeezed her insides, and she slid a hand over her belly.

She was having a baby, and this time, she was surrounded by so much love and support that she'd never have to worry about being alone, struggling, desperate. Never again.

"Thank you, God," she whispered, her eyes burning again. "Thank you for saving me. Thank you for sending me this family and for your love and mercy. I won't forget. I'll never forget."

After an hour of eating, lively discussion, and much laughter, the plates were finally pushed away.

Max cleared his throat and then stood, much as Lily had done at the start of the meal. "I have a surprise for Callie. Well, for everyone," he amended. "It seems even more appropriate in light of all the good news we've recently received. We have much to be grateful for this year. I have the most wonderful, giving wife, and my sister is home where she belongs. Holly is well and back home where she belongs, and now we'll welcome a new addition to the Colter family."

Sounds of agreement echoed on all sides.

"What surprise?" Callie squeaked out.

Max smiled indulgently. "Patience, *dolcezza*. You'll all need to get your coats on and come with me."

Callie grabbed Lauren's hand and dragged her toward the door. Her brothers laughed and shook their heads.

"Come on!" Callie said impatiently. "I'm dying to know what the surprise is!"

Everyone smiled and laughed as they trekked to the closet. Coats were pulled on. Holly was surrounded by her husbands, each of them determined that she wouldn't have to walk solo through the snow. Lily's husbands were every bit as attentive as they stepped outside.

Cold blew over Callie's face and she closed her eyes, inhaling the clean mountain air. Snowflakes danced across her nose and she laughed out loud, mesmerized by the magic of the night.

Max directed them down the pathway that led to her and Max's house. But they stopped in the meadow, halfway between the two houses. He leaned down to kiss Callie, his mouth melting sweetly over the coldness of her lips. Then he drew away and pulled a glow stick from his pocket. After breaking it so that it lit up, he waved it in the air before returning it to his pocket.

There was a silent pause as everyone waited breathlessly. There was anticipation in the air and the only illumination cast on the meadow was the thin slash of moonlight that hovered over distant trees.

Suddenly lights twinkled and lit up, cascading from tree to tree, from bush to bush. Shapes came to life in the meadow. A Christmas tree. Several Christmas trees. Angels. Reindeer. A manger scene.

Callie caught her breath, dazzled by the display of lights, as if a million fireflies had suddenly descended.

"Oh Max," she breathed in a soft voice. "It's magic."

Lauren stood next to Callie, her eyes wide. Everyone seemed transfixed, even Callie's fathers and brothers, who surely were in on the surprise. Her mom stared in wonder, mouth open as she stared from tree to tree.

The meadow had been transformed into a winter wonderland worthy of any childhood fantasy.

In the distance, the sound of sleigh bells chinked softly, growing louder, the rhythm in sync with the trot of horses. Callie whirled around, straining to see. And then a six-horse-drawn sleigh burst into the clearing. The horses were adorned with bells. The sleigh was shiny red, and it reflected the light of thousands of bulbs.

Callie gaped as the sleigh drew even closer. She turned to Max, her mouth working up and down, but nothing would come out. Max chuckled.

Callie flew into his arms, hitting him with such force that they both fell back into the snow. Max's back hit the ground, and he wrapped his arms around her to cushion her fall. He laughed helplessly as she peppered his face with excited, breathless kisses.

Around them, the rest of the family laughed, the sound joyous in the air. Lily clapped her hands in delight and Lauren's smile was so brilliant that it made everyone stop and take notice. How long had it been since she'd really smiled? With everything inside her. With her whole heart.

Gone for a moment were the shadows of her past and in its stead was a beautiful, sparkling young woman.

"Let me up, *dolcezza*. We have a sleigh ride to take."

"All of us?" Callie asked as she got up and literally danced around Max in the snow.

Max stood and brushed the snow from his clothing. "All of us. The sleigh is big enough, and what is Christmas Eve without a sleigh ride?"

"Come on, Lauren!" Callie shouted, taking her sister-in-law's hand and pulling her toward the sleigh.

The rest followed behind and Adam fell into step with Max. "I don't think I've ever seen my little girl so excited."

Max smiled. "I plan to spend the rest of my life making her smile just like she did tonight."

Adam slapped him on the back and then returned to his wife. They ushered her into the sled while Max slid in beside Callie and Lauren. When everyone was tucked underneath the blankets, the man Max had hired to drive the sleigh urged the horses forward.

They glided over the snow, through the meadow, and higher into the aspens and pines that surrounded the Colter cabin. Max wrapped his arm around Callie and pulled her in close. Lauren sat next to Callie, her eyes aglow with happiness.

Everything that mattered most to Max was right here, in his arms, sitting close to him. Seeing Callie's and Lauren's smiles had been worth every bit of planning and money he'd put into having the meadow lit up.

There was nothing more beautiful than the woman resting against his side, and he'd go to hell and back to make her happy. Always. Every damn day for the rest of his life.

CHAPTER 18

CHRISTMAS morning dawned clear and cold. Everyone began to crawl out of bed and make their way downstairs in their pajamas. Ethan had gotten up early to set the fire, and by the time everyone gathered in the living room, flames danced merrily in the hearth.

Snow was coming down harder. Big, fat, fluffy flakes descended, covering the ground in a fresh blanket of white. The windowpanes were frosted over and the women snuggled into the couches with their husbands.

Lauren seemed hesitant to barge in. She paused, feeling a little silly in her pajamas as she stared at the Colter family enjoying cups of hot chocolate while they waited for breakfast to be served.

Then Max looked up, a smile softening his face. He patted the spot beside him and she quickly moved forward, eager and yet afraid all at the same time to find her place in this family Max had married into.

"Hey kiddo," Seth said, leaning over to give her head an affectionate tousle.

She smiled and murmured a greeting before settling back to grip the cup Ryan Colter handed her.

Christmas with the Colters had instilled a fiery ache so deeply rooted that it seemed to take her over completely. She was filled with longing for what they had. Love. Caring. Deep and abiding loyalty.

These men adored their women. Unapologetically. Unabashedly. They didn't give a damn who knew it.

She wanted that. She *deserved* that. It had taken her long enough to believe it, but damn it, she did.

A few minutes later, Adam came in with cinnamon rolls and buttery croissants. Ryan followed with a pitcher of milk as well as juice that he set on the coffee table.

No one was shy about diving right in. It was a

free-for-all that nearly developed into a food fight before Adam eyed his offspring sternly and said, "Now, children."

Lauren found it amusing that even at the Colter children's ages, they immediately snapped to attention and adopted a meek attitude when their father took them to task.

But the good times and teasing resumed, and after they polished off the light breakfast, Holly announced that it was time to open presents.

"I want to be Santa!" Callie exclaimed.

"You can't be Santa. That's the dads' job," Dillon protested.

Callie glared at her brother. "Says who? I want to pass out presents this year."

"Of course you can, baby," Holly said.

"Mama's baby," Dillon mouthed at her.

Callie shot him a smug smile and then scrambled up to start passing out the gifts.

The living room was soon covered in torn wrapping paper, pieces of ribbons, and bows strewn from one end to the other. Everyone oohed and ahhed over each gift, but it was Lily's gift that stole the show.

After everything had been opened, Dillon and his brothers rose, conspiratorial smiles on their faces.

"We have one last gift for Lily," Michael said. "We'll be right back with it."

Lily watched them go, her brow furrowed in confusion. A moment later, they tromped back into the house from outside, shaking the snow from their boots and pajamas.

They carried a blanket-covered object into the living room and placed it front of Lily, and then Dillon carefully pulled the covering away.

Lily gasped as she stared in wonder at the magnificent handcrafted cradle. She knew immediately that Dillon had done this. Probably with his brothers' help.

Her fingers slid over the stained finish with reverence, taking in all the intricate lines and designs that had been carved. But when she got to the end, her vision blurred and she swallowed hard to keep the emotion at bay.

There at the head of the cradle, at the top of the curve, was a simple rose. A gentle remembrance. Letting her know that they hadn't forgotten, that they understood.

She touched it, running her finger over it again and again, so choked up and filled with overwhelming love for her husbands that she couldn't have spoken if she wanted to.

"Thank you," she finally managed to whisper. "It's the most beautiful thing I've ever seen."

Everyone beamed at her, though Holly sniffled and Callie hastily dabbed at her eyes. Even the dads' eyes were suspiciously wet.

"It's a fine piece," Adam proclaimed. "You boys did good."

His declaration lightened the mood and everyone returned to sorting the gifts, collecting the paper, and stacking boxes in a corner.

When all was done, Holly pushed herself up from between Ethan and Adam. "I have an announcement of my own to make."

She stood before her family, a serene smile sliding across her pretty features. Holly Colter reminded Lauren of an angel. The very best kind of angel.

"I'm cooking Christmas dinner today."

There was a series of chokes and wheezes. Spasms crossed the faces of the rest of the Colter family as they tried very hard not to react to her announcement.

Lauren watched them all in puzzlement, not understanding why such an announcement was not only odd but greeted by such an arresting array of responses.

There were even groans. Ryan's face whitened.

Ethan looked panicked. The Colter offspring just dissolved into raucous laughter.

Holly glared at them all, hands on her hips.

"You aren't cooking," Adam said sternly. "You just got out of the hospital."

"Not to mention we don't want her to put *us* in the hospital," Ryan muttered.

Holly scowled at her husband. "I heard that."

"She's a wonderful cook," Lily said, rising to throw her glare in with Holly's.

Holly slid her arm around Lily's waist and beamed at her daughter-in-law. "Thank you, baby."

Ethan sighed and rubbed a hand over his face. Everyone looked like they were preparing to face their executioner.

"Anyone want to hear the menu or shall I just surprise you all?" Holly asked, her eyes brimming with excitement.

Another series of groans echoed over the room.

She pursed her lips and shook her finger at all her naysayers. "You'll see. I'll expect apologies from each and every one of you."

She turned and marched toward the kitchen but stopped midway there to turn and frown at everyone.

"No one better set foot in my kitchen until you're called for dinner. Is that clear?"

"God help us," Adam said wearily.

"*Her* kitchen?" Ethan choked out. "When has it ever been *her* kitchen?"

Feeling compelled to show support for a woman who'd been nothing short of wonderful to her, Lauren stood and fixed the rest of the room with a disapproving frown. "How could you all be so *mean* to her?"

For a moment they all stared at her like she'd lost her mind. Then they dissolved into laughter. Callie wiped at her face and attempted to explain through her merriment.

"We aren't being mean, Lauren. You have to understand. My mom is a disaster in the kitchen."

Seth grimaced. "That's one way to put it."

"She's . . . terrible," Callie went on. "There's no other way to explain her culinary skills, or lack thereof. In the thirty-plus years she and the dads have been together, she's never cooked. It's not that she hasn't occasionally tried, but in an effort to prevent her from burning down the house or poisoning the offspring, the dads banned her from the kitchen."

Another round of laughter filled the room.

With a sigh, Lily shot them all reprimanding looks. "I don't care how awful this meal is, you'll eat it and you'll love it," she said fiercely. "She's worked hard for the last several weeks learning this menu. All she wants is to make Christmas dinner *one* time for her family."

Understanding dawned in Ryan's eyes. "So that's what she's been up to. Hell, we had no idea why she's been sneaking off to your house all the time and refusing to allow us to drive her."

Lily nodded. "We've spent countless hours in the kitchen while she labors over this meal. It's actually quite good. If she doesn't get flustered and can remember everything I taught her, I promise you won't be disappointed."

Adam turned to fix each of his children with a menacing glare. "You'll not say a word to your mother no matter how bad it is. I want her happy, and if making us a meal makes her happy, then by God, we'll sit down and enjoy it even if it kills us."

Ryan coughed and Adam turned his glare on his brother. "That goes for you and Ethan too."

Ethan chuckled.

"There's always leftovers from last night if things go really bad," Callie said.

"Just everyone sit like your mother said and wait for her to come get us," Adam said.

It was hard to sit in the living room when the kitchen might indeed be in peril. Every once in a while, someone could be seen sniffing delicately at the air as if trying to discern whether anything was burning. But after an hour, delicious smells floated through the living room.

At the end of two hours, the smells were so wonderful that the rest of the family began to grow restless and check the time as if they were impatient for dinner to be served.

And then Holly appeared in the doorway of the living room, her smile triumphant even if she looked decidedly harried and bedraggled.

"Dinner is served," she declared, her smile bright enough to rival the meadow the night before.

Everyone scrambled up and jockeyed for position going into the dining room. It was as if they all wanted to be the first to see the results of Holly's cooking.

When they all crowded into the doorway, exclamations and sounds of surprise rose. The table was set with a red tablecloth and a beautiful poinsettia centerpiece. Each place was set with sterling silver utensils and Holly had dragged out her rarely used fine china for the occasion.

But what everyone focused in on was the mouth-wateringly fragrant food.

"Sit, sit," she urged. "I don't want it to get cold."

Neither did anyone else.

They scrambled into their seats and discovered steaming bowls of lobster bisque accompanied by an appetizer of crawfish-stuffed shrimp. Homemade rolls were passed around and then silence descended as everyone glanced around to see who would be the first to try it.

Max didn't hold back, but then he'd never been a victim of Holly's attempts at cooking. He spooned a mouthful of the bisque into his mouth and then took a bite of the hot roll.

He looked up when he realized everyone was staring at him. He laughed. "I suppose I could pretend to keel over and die an agonizing death, but that would probably get me banned from any future family meals."

"Damn right it would," Holly muttered.

"It's excellent, Mrs. C.," Max said. "You outdid yourself."

The others looked surprised and then suddenly they

were all dipping into their bowls and the reactions were comical.

"Oh my God, this is heaven," Ethan groaned. "My wife made this?"

Holly huffed at him and shot him a quick glare.

No one spoke for a long moment as they all savored the wonderful-tasting bisque. When they all finished, Holly began dishing up the grilled fish fillets. When she opened the covered bowl containing the étouffée, there were looks of amazement all around.

She carefully ladled the étouffée onto the plates, covering the fillets.

"What the hell did you do to our mother?" Dillon demanded as he forked another bite into his mouth.

The entire table cracked up at his irreverence. Even Holly grinned. "You like?"

"Like? I damn well love," Dillon said around another mouthful. "Did my wife teach you how to make all this?"

Holly shot a proud glance in Lily's direction. "She sure did."

Adam, Ethan, and Ryan all looked over at Lily, and Ethan said in mock reverence, "How can we ever thank you? You've performed a miracle. We never thought we'd see the day she didn't burn the house down after two hours in the kitchen."

"Oh, shut up," Holly said in exasperation. "I'm not that bad!"

When silence greeted her defensive statement, she burst into laughter. "Okay, so maybe I was."

"Everything is wonderful, baby," Adam said with a smile. "You did an amazing job. This will be a Christmas we'll never forget for many reasons."

Holly smiled back at him, her cheeks flushed with pleasure.

"It's awesome, Mom," Seth assured her.

One by one, her children and her husbands, Max, and Lauren all chimed in with their compliments until Holly beamed from ear to ear, and really, even if it had been horrible, who would have wanted to wipe away that kind of smile?

It had been a year of many milestones and events, changes and renewals, scares and rejoicings. The next year promised to be even sweeter.

But no matter what else would be recounted from this point forward, this would always be remembered as the year Holly Colter finally managed to conquer the kitchen.

TURN THE PAGE FOR
A SPECIAL PREVIEW OF

ECHOES AT DAWN

THE NEXT KGI NOVEL FROM
MAYA BANKS,
COMING JULY 2012 FROM
BERKLEY SENSATION!

GRACE Peterson drew the blanket tighter around her and huddled in the dark. She stared blankly at the star-filled sky. The mountain air was cold. Not just chilly, as it had been as dusk had descended, wiping away the comfortable remnants of a sunny afternoon. It was frigid.

A low moan escaped as her muscles tightened and protested not only the cold, but the weakness inflicted upon them by so much death and sickness. Pain had long since lost any meaning to her. What she felt couldn't really be considered pain. It was worse. She couldn't feel anything but the desolation of hopelessness and despair. The knowledge that she would probably die from the horrors inflicted upon her. And perhaps she deserved it, for she hadn't been able to help all who had been thrust upon her.

Her escape had been a fluke. An explosion had decimated the cell where she'd been held. She'd managed to get out before the men charged with her care had been able to respond. Or maybe they had perished. She couldn't bring herself to feel any regret. They'd shown her no regard. She'd been treated like an inanimate object. Some magic wand they waved at a wound or an illness and expected her to make it all disappear.

She hated them for that. Hated them for their callousness. For using others as they'd used her. Pawns. Objects to provide them with information. They weren't even people. Just numbers.

Another shiver rattled her teeth and settled deep into her bones. She simply couldn't imagine ever being warm again. She curled her feet further into the blanket and tucked the ends securely under her chin.

She was severely weakened by all she'd been forced to endure. For all she'd been made to heal. Even now she didn't know where she'd found the strength or the will to make her escape when the opportunity had presented itself.

But now she'd run out of strength. She had nothing else left. No reserves. And her resolve was faltering just as everything else had done.

Closing her eyes, she tried to find some solace. Some measure of peace.

She missed her sister, Shea. Ached for the comfort of her touch. The brush of her mind and the image of her smile. She hadn't ever really understood and hadn't ever taken Shea's decision for them to separate seriously. Until the day she'd been captured, and she realized that if they'd been together, they would have both been taken.

Shea had always been determined to keep Grace safe, but now, Grace was equally determined to keep Shea as far away from her as possible. Grace was hunted. She knew her pursuers were probably in these mountains already. They could be a short distance away.

And so she'd slammed the door shut on her sister, and the void hurt every bit as much as the bombardment of sickness and pain she'd absorbed. Not having Shea there was the worst sort of loneliness. She'd severed the telepathic link between her and her sister, and her worst fear was that it was permanent. She'd never get it back.

In a way, she supposed it would be a blessing. If she lost her abilities, she could have a normal life. But so would she lose the ability to make a difference in someone else's life.

She closed her eyes, exhausted by the weight of responsibility, sorrow, and regret. She hated that she wasn't stronger, that she'd crumbled under so much stress. But the ailments had been thrown at her, one after another. Broken bones, horrible bloody wounds, tumors, diseases, and the list went on and on. The most horrific experiment she'd undergone was when it had been demanded of her to reach inside the mind of a woman with a mental illness and heal her.

For three long days Grace had known what it truly was to be insane. She'd lived the woman's existence while the woman had gone away, cleansed of the darkness in her brain. Twice, Grace had tried to kill herself, not because it was what she wanted, but because it was what the illness dictated. In the end, she'd been restrained, unable to do even the basic necessities for herself because the fear had been too great that she'd find a way to end her life.

She was hungry, but the thought of food made her stomach twist into knots. She drånk water from nearby streams frequently, because she knew she had to do something to keep her strength up. And no matter that she bore the knowledge that she would likely die, she couldn't bring herself to simply give up. Not yet.

Quietly, she turned over, rearranging the blanket in the fruitless hope she'd somehow find greater warmth. Eventually she'd have to reach out to her sister, but if she did so now, Shea would see the horrific shape Grace was in. Shea would come. She'd put herself in grave danger. Grace would never be able to live with herself if Shea was sacrificed because in a moment of weakness Grace gave in and tried to re-establish the link with her sister.

Silent tears slid down Grace's cheeks, briefly warming her skin until the chilly air turned them to ice. She angrily scrubbed them away and hunched lower, furious with herself for allowing despair to control her.

She was stronger than this, and she'd be strong again. She just needed time to recover from her ordeal. Maybe she'd never be the same as she was, but she wasn't going to give in. If she died, she'd die running. She'd die standing up and fighting. She refused to die in some laboratory where rats were treated with less disdain.

A distant sound froze her to the bone. She went so still that even her breath sounded like a roar in the night. She pushed the blanket over her mouth, trying to quell the noise, and she stared into the trees, trying desperately to see through the thick curtain of night.

Someone was coming.

THEY crawled through the mountains under the cover of dark. Rio knew they were close. They'd been closing in on Grace for days now, but somehow she'd managed to elude them just when he was sure they'd come upon her.

He trilled a soft bird call, and several yards away, an answering call returned. He adjusted his pack, slipped on the infrared goggles and scanned the area ahead, looking for anything giving off a heat signal.

There were several smaller forms. Animals. Even a larger shape that must have been an elk or a deer. Nothing that resembled a human, though.

He'd given orders for strict radio silence. They weren't the only ones who sought Grace. But he was determined to get to her first. His gut told him they needed to catch up to her before dawn. The hairs on his nape rose and apprehension slipped down his spine. It wasn't that he feared confrontation. In truth, he'd savor killing the bastards who'd made Grace and Shea's life hell over the last year.

It was the knowledge that she was in danger and that he and his men needed to end this game of cat and mouse.

Beside him, Terrence, his right hand, melted into the dark just a few feet away. Rio continued a path further up the mountain. There were any number of nooks and crannies a small woman could hide and so he carefully scanned the area, looking for any heat source.

Where are you, Grace? I know you're here. I can feel you.

And it was true. There was a distinct prickle, the same awareness he'd experienced the first time he'd seen her on the surveillance footage. The last time anyone had seen her before she'd disappeared.

He'd known beyond a shadow of a doubt that he would be the one to go after her and bring her back to her sister. Safe and alive.

Since that time, he'd tracked her movements with uncanny accuracy. He and his men hadn't left a stone unturned in their search for her. They'd gone back to the house where she'd last been seen and had broadened their search from there.

It had taken weeks, but now they were following a lead into the mountains of Colorado and Rio was sure they were close. His gut was screaming and he never ignored his gut. It had kept him alive more times than he could count.

He paused when he heard a noise in the distance. He turned, scanning the area, and then he saw the infrared images of men he knew weren't his moving stealthily through the trees.

Damn it.

He curled his hand into a fist. Where the hell was Grace? He didn't have time to play hide-and-seek with the men who were after her. He needed to grab her and get the hell out.

He pulled his rifle from over his shoulder and silently moved in the direction of the heat signature. Ideally he didn't want to shoot up the whole damn mountain and leave bodies lying everywhere. He'd rather find Grace and make a stealthy exit, but the savage part of him relished spilling a little blood.

A cry in the night froze him momentarily. He lifted his head to capture the faint echo as it died in the distance. It was a feminine cry, one that sent chills chasing down his spine. There was a hell of a lot of anguish, pain, and fear in that one small sound.

Grace.

He began to run, closing in on the source of the noise. He ripped the goggles from his head, needing to see his surroundings better. A hundred yards ahead, Terrence fell in beside him and they charged the remaining distance, guns up and ready.

They slowed when they reached the edge of a drop-off that overlooked a small valley below. The moon shone down, reflecting off the smooth rock floor and Rio's gut clenched as he saw Grace Peterson backed to a steep edge that plummeted hundreds of feet into a riverbed.

He sensed the grim determination in her that she wouldn't be captured again. He knew without doubt that she'd jump before ever going back. Her fear and desolation was like a tangible scent in the air. It tightened every one of his muscles, gripped his heart and squeezed relentlessly.

He had to get to her before the idiots forced her over with their stupidity.

Dropping down onto his belly, he pulled his gun up and put the crosshairs on the man closest to Grace.

The stupid fuck had his hand held out in a placating manner but in his other hand was a gun and it was pointed directly at Grace. His entire posture screamed menace.

Rio squeezed a shot off. The man dropped like a stone and suddenly his comrades hit the ground and turned in the direction of the gunfire.

"Hell," Terrence muttered as he got into position. "Thought we weren't engaging?"

"Cover me. I'm going in," Rio bit out.

Before Terrence could protest, Rio scrambled over the edge and rapidly worked his way down until he reached bottom. Above him, Terrence squeezed off round after round, the sounds echoing harshly in the night.

They had a limited amount of time before someone came to investigate all the gunfire. He turned and immediately searched for Grace again. To his horror he found her just as the edge gave way under her feet and she plummeted over the side.

He lunged forward as more gunfire erupted. This time, Terrence wasn't trying to scare them. They dropped like flies as Terrence put them down one by one as Rio flew to the edge.

Trusting his man to protect his back, Rio only

focused on trying to see how far down Grace had fallen or if the worst had occurred and she'd gone the entire distance to the riverbed.

He dug a flashlight out of his pack and dropped to his belly. He pointed the light down and made a slow sweep. As he pulled it closer to the side of the cliff, the light bounced over a tattered sneaker. He yanked the light up to see Grace lying limply on an outcropping. Her feet dangled over the side and her slim form barely fit the ledge. But she hadn't fallen more than twenty feet.

Breaking radio silence, he called for immediate assistance. His men would have to lower him over by rope and he'd have to haul Grace up over his shoulder. Provided she was still alive. He wouldn't consider any alternative, though. She hadn't made it this far to go quietly.

As he was pushing to his knees, Terrence dropped down beside him, flashing his own light over the side.

"Diego and Browning have our sixes. Decker and Alton are scrambling to get here," Terrence said. "I'll lower you over with rope so you can get Grace."

"All dead?"

"All dead," Terrence confirmed.

Rio couldn't waste time lamenting the mess they'd

made. Grace was the priority and then they had to get the hell out of here before everything went to shit.

Terrence yanked out a coil of rope with a rappel hook on the end and quickly fastened it around his waist. He took several steps back, dug his heels into the soil and then wrapped the extra length around the base of an aspen and set the hook into the bark. He tossed the other end to Rio.

Rio secured the flashlight to his leg, pointing downward so his descent would be illuminated. Then he secured the end of the rope around his waist, yanked to make sure it was securely knotted, and then edged backward until his heels hung over the side.

Just before he started downward, Decker and Alton hit the scene. They rushed past Diego and Browning, who were standing watch, and each grabbed one of Rio's hands to help him over the side.

They leaned down as he made his descent, holding onto his wrists until he had sure footing and he was certain that Terrence could support his weight.

The light bounced crazily as he continued downward. He glanced over his shoulder to see Grace still lying on the small ledge. He just hoped to hell it held both their weight.

He pushed off the side of the cliff when he reached her and lowered himself enough that he straddled the outcropping. Immediately he pressed his fingers to her neck, feeling for her pulse, and was reassured by the steady thud.

"Grace. Wake up. I've come to get you out of here but I need your help here."

When he didn't receive a response, his lips tightened in frustration. At the top, Decker and Browning shone their lights down. He dug his feet into the side, finding purchase, and then he carefully let go of the rope to slide his arms underneath her limp body.

Mentally counting to three, he hoisted her up and then arranged her over one shoulder so he could hold the rope with a free hand. He held her tightly, his arm a steel band over the backs of her legs.

"Pull us up," he called up to his teammates.

Toe over toe, he dug into the side as the rope inched higher. His muscles bulged with the strain of bearing both their weight. The rope cut into his skin and his fingers were numb from his grip.

Let me die. Please.

At first he thought she'd said it aloud. It startled him into stillness. His toes dragged as they hoisted him higher and he had to scramble to regain his footing and assist them as they pulled him and Grace the remaining way.

He was suddenly swamped with desolation so acute that he couldn't breathe. Pain. Fear. Regret. Hopelessness. And weariness that went soul deep.

He knew then that he'd heard Grace's innermost thoughts. He was feeling what she felt. And her sorrow was so great that it staggered him.

Her tears were locked inside her, but he felt each one. Memories of all she'd endured flashed through his mind until he had to close his eyes to control his reeling senses.

I won't go back.

Her voice whispered through his mind, so broken that he wanted to bellow in rage. He wanted to crawl up over the side of this damn cliff and rip apart the savages who'd pursued her so relentlessly and kill them all over again. The men who'd broken her spirit and made her even now want to die rather than endure more.

He knew that Nathan Kelly had been able to communicate with Grace's sister, Shea, telepathically, but he hadn't considered how or that he and Grace might be able to communicate the same way. It hadn't been important at the time. He'd been gripped by the urgency to find her and keep her safe. Nothing else had mattered at that moment.

Tentatively, he reached out with his mind and spoke gently and reassuringly to her.

You'll never go back to those bastards, Grace. You're safe now. I'm here to help you. Don't give up. You'll get through this.

There was nothing but silence and he clenched his jaw in frustration. How the hell did you communicate with your mind? How did he even know if he was able to talk to her the same way she'd just spoken to him? He didn't even know if she was cognizant of the fact that he'd picked up on those desperate thoughts.

His teammates' faces came into view as he neared the edge. Their expressions were tense as they hauled him the remaining distance. Diego pushed forward while Decker and Browning held tight to the rope and he took Grace from Rio's grasp.

Free of her weight, Rio hoisted himself over the side and he rolled to his feet. Terrence let out a light huff, his only indication of the toll the rescue had taken on him. Rio quickly untied the rope and issued orders for his men to dispose of the bodies and then to be prepared to bug out.

They were in the middle of nowhere, no backup, no helo, their vehicles at least two miles away.

He strode to where Diego had laid Grace carefully on the ground and he dropped to his knees beside her.

He pushed the hair out of her face with gentle fingers and frowned at the deep shadows under her eyes, the paleness of her features, and the deep lines of fatigue etched into her forehead. Her expression was grim even in unconsciousness.

Not knowing what possessed him, he found himself leaning down to press his lips to her forehead.

You don't give up, Grace. You're safe now. I won't hurt you and I won't allow anyone else to do so either. I'm going to take you home.

SUNLIGHT warmed her face, though she was in the grip of a pervasive chill that was bone deep. It hurt to shiver and yet she couldn't do anything else.

It was as if there were weights pressing over her eyelids, preventing them from opening. Or perhaps she simply lacked the strength to do the simplest tasks anymore.

Pain crept over her, through her, puzzling her with its intensity. It was new. Fresh. And then she remembered falling over the side, sure that death had finally come to claim her.

A soft moan escaped before she could call it back and she chastised herself for that momentary loss of control. Such a lapse could get her killed.

Grace. Grace.

It took her a moment to realize that the person calling her name wasn't saying it aloud but in her mind. She recoiled, wanting nothing to do with the distant voice. And then she was surrounded by strength. Warmth. It flooded into her veins so comforting that it shook her to her core.

"Grace."

This time it was said aloud. A deep, rough, slightly accented voice. Just a hint of another world, one she couldn't place.

"Wake up, Grace. Let me see those gorgeous baby blues."

Her brow wrinkled and she tried to process her surroundings. She was afraid to open her eyes. Afraid that she'd be right back in the hands of monsters, forced to do their bidding. The mere thought made her want to weep. She wasn't strong enough to endure more.

A gentle hand stroked over her cheek and carefully

pushed away her hair, tucking it over her ear. Such warmth and tenderness. It was like rain to a sun-parched desert. She soaked it up, desperate for any comfort.

It took everything she had to conquer her fear and open her eyes. Sunlight stabbed through her vision, momentarily blinding her.

"That's it," the man said in a low voice. "Come back to me, Grace. I need you to wake up so we can figure out how badly you're hurt."

At the mere mention of injuries, pain screamed through her body. Her eyes flew open and her lips parted. Her breath rushed out, her chest jerking violently with the effort.

Fear nearly paralyzed her when her gaze met with the dark eyes of a man staring intently at her. She let out a cry and tried to bolt, not even realizing that he was still holding her.

She tumbled to the ground, landing with a thud that knocked the breath from her and sent agony tearing through her body again.

The man above her cursed vehemently and he immediately knelt beside her, running those big hands over her fragile body.

"Damn it, Grace, I'm not going to hurt you."

"I won't go back."

She barely managed to stammer out the defiant vow. It hurt to talk. It hurt to breathe. She felt broken. Something was broken. Her ribs, an arm . . . She couldn't even decipher what was wrong with her. There was simply too much to process.

She stared up at him in panic, knowing she didn't possess the strength to escape. Tears gathered at the corners of her eyes. She could do nothing to *prevent* him from taking her back.

A deep shudder rolled through her body and the tears that had threatened slowly slid down her cheeks.

"Grace, I want you to listen to me."

His voice was calm and oddly soothing. The tone mesmerized her as did those dark eyes that refused to look away from her.

"My name is Rio. I've come to take you home. To Shea."

Her pulse leapt and her throat tightened. "Shea?" she croaked. "Is she all right?"

What if it was a trap? What if he was using information about her sister to lull her into a false sense of security?

He touched her cheek, his fingers infinitely gentle on her skin. He didn't look like a man who had an ounce of gentleness in him. He was big and menacing. A warrior.

Dark-skinned, like he'd spent many hours in the sun, uncaring of the consequences. His hair was pulled back into a ponytail at his nape and his eyes were as dark as night.

"I spoke to her myself," he soothed. "I promised her I'd find you and protect you. We're the good guys, Grace. I realize you may have a hard time believing that or trusting me, but we're here to help you. Shea is safe and she wants very much to see you again. We've all been worried about you."

More tears slid down her cheeks and a quiet sob hiccupped from her throat. "I don't want her to see me like this."

Something like understanding flashed in his eyes. He touched her face again, wiping at the moisture on her cheekbone.

"I need you to tell me where you're hurt. We have to move you. We can't stay in this location, but I need to know what we risk by moving you more than we already have."

She glanced around, slowly taking in her surroundings for the first time. Her breath caught when she saw the others. Warriors. Like this man called Rio.

Stern and forbidding. How was she to know she could trust them? What choice did she have?

They were away from where she'd fallen the night before. How had they managed to find her and how had she survived the fall? Her memory of the event was hazy. She could only remember that moment when she knew she would likely die.

She'd thought that a lot lately. Pondered her mortality as calmly as she might consider what shoes to wear. And yet she was here and alive. Broken but not defeated.

The men were facing away from where she and Rio were positioned. Watchful and wary. Guns up, their stances rigid as if they sensed danger in the very air.

"Grace," Rio prompted. "Talk to me. I need to know how bad it is."

She briefly closed her eyes and then reopened them, focusing once more on his face. She licked her lips. "I hurt."

"I know you do," he said quietly.

"The fall. I think I broke something."

She centered her attention on her body, paying attention to where she hurt and how it differed from the residual pain of the endless torture she'd endured. Her breaths were strained. Shallow and painful.

"Ribs," she managed to gasp out. "Think I have broken ribs. And my arm. It hurts but it's growing numb. I can't feel my fingers."

"Yes, I can see," Rio said as he carefully picked up her hand.

He turned his head and nodded at one of the men. She tensed when the big burly man closest to Rio hovered over her. He was a mountain. Arms bulging with muscles. He barely had a neck as thick as he was. Legs like tree trunks.

"She's lost feeling in her fingers," Rio said as if discussing something as mundane as the weather. "We'll have to set the break."

Her pulse exploded and she tried to sit up but Rio put a hand on her shoulder. "Be still, Grace."

The command in his voice froze her in her tracks.

"Can you heal yourself?"

The idle curiosity in his voice baffled her. He was so calm. Unruffled. He spoke of her abilities like they were the most natural things in the world. She glanced nervously between the two men, wondering if this was some kind of trap, though she couldn't imagine what it could be.

The people who'd kept her captive knew well her

abilities. They wouldn't have to ask questions. Was this yet another faction who wanted to use her?

Panic was rising swiftly when Rio simply put his hand on her cheek and softly caressed. "Take deep breaths, okay? We're going to help you. This is Terrence. He's my second in command. That's Diego right behind him. Diego acts as our medic when Donovan Kelly isn't around to patch us up, but Terrence is going to set the break for you."

Her brow wrinkled in confusion. She had no idea who any of these people were but Rio continued a steady stream of conversation, ignoring her befuddlement.

"This is going to hurt like a son of a bitch. I won't lie to you. But I need you to be strong. If you scream, you'll draw attention and that's the last thing we need. I'm going to knot one of my shirts, and I want you to bite down on it as hard as you like. But don't let out a sound. Can you do that?"

If he only knew how much she'd silently endured, he'd never ask that question. But she simply nodded, knowing that whatever they did wouldn't touch what she'd already gone through.

He took out a T-shirt from his pack and began

folding and knotting it into a long rope. "You didn't answer my question. Can you heal yourself as you do others?"

"Yes," she whispered. "I mean it's different, but I do heal faster. But there's been so much . . ." She closed her eyes, holding back more tears. "I don't know . . . "

Rio spoke in low, soothing tones. "It's okay, Grace. I'm going to make sure you get out of this okay."

Something in his voice settled her. Maybe it was the calm promise or the absolute conviction. Some of the fear faded and she relaxed, letting out her breath in a whispery rush.

"That's my girl," Rio murmured.

He carefully placed the shirt between her teeth, feathered his hand over her jaw and then eased her mouth shut over the material.

"Be strong."

She closed her eyes and nodded, not wanting to see what was coming.

Strong hands gripped her arm in a surprisingly gentle manner. She could instantly tell the difference, knew that it was Terrence who held her hand.

And then he simply pulled and twisted, all at the same time. His strength took her completely by surprise. Her eyes flew open and her teeth bit savagely into the shirt. Her body bowed with the instant flash of pain. As she lay panting, her nostrils flaring with the ragged breaths she tried to suck in, a sense of relief settled over her.

Her arm ached from the manipulation, but the constant red hot pain had subsided. Diego stepped in and quickly bound her arm, using two sturdy saplings one of the other men had fetched. He wound strips of cloth tightly around the sticks so it was impossible for her to move her arm.

Rio pulled the knotted shirt from her mouth. "Better?"

She nodded, still not trusting herself to speak.

"Okay, this is what's going to happen. We have to move and I can't spare the manpower necessary to keep you immobile. We don't have a stretcher, which means I'm going to carry you out while my men surround us and provide cover. With a broken arm and ribs plus God only knows what else you've got going on, there's no easy way to do this. It's going to suck."

She tried to smile at the blunt way he put it but her lips trembled and she gave up with a sigh.

"I'll need at least one hand free so I can hold a gun and protect us both. Terrence will secure you to my back. We once carried a teammate's wife out of the jungle just like I'm going to carry you, so it'll work. I don't want you to worry. If you don't trust in anything else, you trust in the fact that we're going to get you out of these mountains."

The unwavering conviction in his voice gave her the first hope she'd experienced in many weeks.

"I won't let you give up," Rio continued. "I know you hurt. I can only imagine what those bastards did to you. But you aren't giving up, Grace. You're a fighter. Your sister's a fighter."

Tears shimmered in her vision again, making Rio grow hazy. "I can't talk to her. I'm not sure I can talk to anyone . . . like before I mean."

Rio leaned over, his face close to hers. "You'll get it back. I heard you last night. It's there. You just have to heal both in body and spirit."

"Who are you?" she whispered around the knot in her throat.

He smiled then, white teeth flashing against dark skin. "I'm the man who's going to get you the hell out of here and then I'm going to hunt down those sons of bitches who hurt you and gut every last one of them."

She shivered at the menace in his voice but was oddly comforted by the savage vow.

"We need to roll, Rio," Terrence said, startling her. She'd forgotten his presence. Had forgotten all of the men standing in close proximity.

Rio nodded and then stood, towering over her. She suddenly felt very small and insignificant and extremely vulnerable as she lay huddled on the ground, surrounded by the warriors with death in their eyes.

This time Terrence knelt by her side, his voice quiet and she suspected purposely gentle so as not to scare the bejebus out of her. It was a little late for that . . .

"All right, Miss Grace. This is what's going to happen. The men are going to fashion a sling of sorts that will secure you to Rio's back. I'm going to lift you very carefully. I'll try not to hurt you."

She nodded her understanding.

He smiled at her, and she decided he was an extremely handsome man despite his fierce appearance. Moreover, she believed him when he said he'd try not to hurt her.

He slid his arms underneath her body. "Deep breath."

She sucked in, closed her eyes and he lifted upward.

She was amazed at the ease in which he picked her up. She opened her eyes and watched him. There was no evident strain. Just calm focus.

Diego appeared on her other side.

"Diego's going to hook his arm underneath your leg," Terrence explained. "I'm going to take the other."

She appreciated the patience he demonstrated and how he explained every step so she wouldn't be frightened. At this point, she was ready to be done with it all. The sooner they left this place where she was hunted, the better she'd feel. Maybe then she could begin healing.

She nodded her acceptance and as soon as she did, Diego stepped forward and slid his arm underneath her legs. He hooked his other arm behind her and he and Terrence held her up to Rio's back.

The other two men quickly wound the long strips of cloth they'd secured together underneath her bottom and underneath her legs. They did a series of figure eights, coiling rope and material up and over Rio's shoulders then under and around her legs and behind until she was solidly supported and attached to his back.

Diego positioned her splinted arm at Rio's side just

underneath his armpit and then secured it to Rio's body as well.

She had no idea how on earth Rio was going to be able to move with her plastered to his body the way she was, much less carry a gun, but he didn't seem at all bothered by the prospect.

"How are the ribs?" Rio asked.

"Okay."

"They'll hurt when he starts walking," Diego warned. "Try to press against him to minimize your movements as much as possible. The more you jostle, the more it's going to cause you pain."

She nodded again and pressed in as close to Rio as she could get. Already she was exhausted and they hadn't even begun the journey out. She didn't even know how far they had to travel and she didn't want to ask because she wasn't sure she could handle the answer.

Instead she was going to put herself in their hands because she had no other choice. She had no idea who these men were—only that they knew her sister and they professed to want to help her.

She'd been prepared to die. It shamed her that she'd been so ready to give in. At her absolute lowest point, these men had appeared, refusing to let her give up.

Rio had promised to take her home, though she had no inkling of what home meant. She'd spent too much time on the run, separated from her only family.

The idea that she was finally safe and could see her sister after so long was more than she could comprehend.

"Ready, Grace?" Rio called over his shoulder.

She took a deep breath, realizing that she was venturing into the unknown once again. Only this time she wasn't alone and that bolstered her flagging resolve like nothing else could.

"Ready."

The Promise of Love

SIX ORIGINAL STORIES EDITED BY *NEW YORK TIMES* BESTSELLING AUTHOR

Lori Foster

INCLUDING NOVELLAS FROM

LORI FOSTER   ERIN MCCARTHY   SYLVIA DAY
JAMIE DENTON   KATE DOUGLAS   KATHY LOVE

Six award-winning and bestselling authors present a never-before-published anthology touching upon the obstacles people confront in their lives—and those who help heal their hearts.

These stories feature women who are survivors of stormy pasts, and the good men who have become stronger for understanding them. Together they can overcome anything, with a love born of compassion...

From #1 *New York Times* Bestselling Author

LORA LEIGH

and National Bestselling Author

JACI BURTON

NAUTI AND WILD

Two all-new novellas of the games men and women play between chrome and hot leather.

Lora Leigh revisits her sultry Southern landscape with a story of a good girl gone bad. But she's not the only one going down that road . . .

Jaci Burton writes the story of a hot biker hired to keep an eye on the reckless daughter of a Nevada senator. She's hooked up with a rival biker gang— a dangerous move that makes the wild beauty more vulnerable than she imagined . . .

penguin.com

M698T0510

Finally!
Classic Nora Roberts novels available as eBooks for the first time!

Nora Roberts' popular characters—the O'Hurleys, the Donovans, and the Cordinas—are going digital for the very first time. Now, with just a few clicks, readers can experience the engaging family dynamics, the powerful friendships, and the thrilling passion that Nora brings to life in her bestselling novels.

The O'Hurleys
THE LAST HONEST WOMAN

DANCE TO THE PIPER

SKIN DEEP

WITHOUT A TRACE

The Donovan Legacy
CAPTIVATED

ENTRANCED

CHARMED

ENCHANTED

Cordina's Royal Family
AFFAIRE ROYALE

COMMAND PERFORMANCE

THE PLAYBOY PRINCE

CORDINA'S CROWN JEWEL

Look for a new selection of classic Nora Roberts titles available throughout 2012!

noraroberts.com
facebook.com/noraroberts
penguin.com/intermix

LOVE
ROMANCE
NOVELS?

For news on all your favorite romance authors,
sneak peeks into the newest releases, book
giveaways, and much more—

"Like" Love Always on Facebook!
 LoveAlwaysBooks

M1063G0212